THE SECRET HO

They sat, side by side, on the veranda, and each
time they inhaled their cigarettes they could see
each other's faces in the red glow of the burning
ends. When Shane had lit Evelyn's cigarette for
her, his little finger touched hers, and a queer,
electric current ran between them. Why? Who
can tell? Who can solve the mystery of mutual
attraction? Evelyn mused that some men mean
nothing to a woman in a year and others can
mean much in a moment. Such a man was
Shane Cargill.

**Also by the same author,
and available in Coronet Books:**

Put Back The Clock
And All Because
To Love is To Live
The Cyprus Love Affair
Forbidden
House Of The Seventh Cross
The Boundary Line
Love Was A Jest
The Noble One
Laurence, My Love
Gay Defeat
Do Not Go My Love
All For You
I Should Have Known
The Unlit Fire
Shatter The Sky
The Strong Heart
Once is Enough
The Other Side Of Love
This Spring of Love
We Two Together
The Story of Veronica
Wait for Tomorrow
Love and Desire and Hate
A Love Like Ours
Mad Is the Heart
Sweet Cassandra
To Love Again
The Crash
Arrow in the Heart
A Promise is Forever
Stranger Than Fiction
     Autobiography)

The Secret Hour

Denise Robins

CORONET BOOKS
Hodder and Stoughton

Copyright Denise Robins
First published in Great Britain 1932 by Mills & Boon

Coronet edition 1976

Printed and bound in Great Britain for
Coronet Books, Hodder and Stoughton, London,
By Richard Clay (The Chaucer Press), Ltd.,
Bungay, Suffolk

ISBN 0 340 19931 8

THE SECRET HOUR

I

The swift darkness had fallen—that hot, close darkness which descends upon the glittering day in South Africa.

Evelyn Mayton, sitting on the veranda of the Embassy Hotel, Johannesburg, felt something more than the darkness closing about her. She lifted her eyes from a letter which she had been reading and looked over the exotic garden with almost a fatalistic expression on her young, lovely face.

'Life,' she whispered. 'What are you offering me? What is there in store? A husband—money—security for father and me—but what of love—and a lover?'

What indeed! There was a restless, tormented feeling in the heart of Evelyn to-night. She looked again at the last paragraph of the letter which had come out from England and reached her this morning. A letter from her father, from their home in London.

'And now that I know the date of your wedding with Gordon is fixed, I have no further worries. Thank heavens he fell in love with you and you with him. You will be happy, won't you, my little girl? I couldn't bear you to do this thing for my sake alone....'

Evelyn turned her eyes to the darkness again. Her lips—red, exquisitely shaped, with a short, passionate upper lip—twisted into a smile. Not a happy smile for a girl of twenty-one who is just about to be married. Her restless, tormented feeling increased.

'Poor father!' she whispered. 'If he knew how little I am in love—how little I want my marriage——'

A few months ago she had been living with her father in town, leading the ordinary life of a carefree, attractive girl, with exceptional beauty and, so far as outsiders knew, with money behind her.

Her mother was dead. Ever since she was fifteen Evelyn had been all in all to her father and adored him. It had come as a considerable shock to her to discover that he was badly pressed for money, and that in a moment of weakness he had borrowed a considerable sum on forged security from a man named Gordon Veriland, a diamond merchant with whom he had had business dealings.

Veriland had discovered what Charles Mayton had done. But he had neither reproached nor condemned. He was a curious character. Domineering, stubborn—immensely selfish. He had met Evelyn. Her fair, slender beauty and her intriguing personality had at once fascinated him. He was forty; just the age to fall crazily in love. He wanted Evelyn for his wife. He asked her to marry him. It was all very subtle. No mention was made of her father's folly. But Evelyn knew—knew that if she accepted Gordon Veriland that crime would be wiped out, and she and her father need never worry about money again.

Veriland sailed for South Africa in a hurry on urgent business. One month later Evelyn followed as his future wife. She had given her word. And in a fashion she liked him. He was not repellent to her. He had a certain amount of personal attraction—a good figure, good features—and he was literally at her feet.

So here she was—and in a week's time Gordon would be here and they would be married. She was waiting for him. Her trousseau was ready—her future settled and assured. Gordon was up-country at his famous mine and he wrote to her every day. Only this morning she had had one of his notes—brief but possessive in every line.

Evelyn shut her eyes. Slim, lovely, fair as a man's dream of real English beauty, with her pale gold hair curled at the nape of her neck, her grey, black-lashed eyes, her rose-petal skin, she looked about seventeen in her white linen dress. A slender, rather fragile girl. And she ought to have been on fire with love—with the thrill of what was to come next week when she became Gordon's wife. But the thrill was missing—so far as he was concerned. Not once had Evelyn—the real Evelyn—wakened to her fiancé's kiss or touch. His lovemaking even bored her a little.

She knew that the real thing had not come.

To-night she stretched out white arms and whispered:

'Life—what are you offering me?'

A big grey car with strong headlights came at a reckless pace round the curve in the hotel drive and stopped. It stood there, throbbing like a live creature, just in front of the veranda where Evelyn was sitting.

She stood up, and the wistfulness in her grey eyes changed to a peculiar look of interest.

A man stepped out of the grey car and came up the white steps towards her. She knew he had seen her. In the glaring headlights she recognised him. Shane Cargill, like herself, was a visitor at the

7

Embassy Hotel. Only last night Evelyn heard him discussed by a woman in the lounge:

'Shane Cargill is the wickedest, nicest man in South Africa—an absolute devil—breaks the hearts of all the women he meets——'

That was enough to intrigue any girl, and Evelyn, at heart most romantic, was no exception. She became interested in the 'wickedest, nicest man in South Africa.' She found out a little more about him. He was a bachelor of considerable means and one of this world's rovers. He spent his time in travelling—big-game hunting was his chief passion, and, so Evelyn's informant said, pretty women.

Evelyn was amused. Certainly Shane was very handsome, and there was a little dare-devil, arrogant smile generally playing about his well-shaped lips when he strolled through the lounge. A smile that seemed to say:

'Come on—if you dare—I challenge you!'

Evelyn liked being challenged. She wished she could speak to Shane Cargill—and see what he was really like.

He collided with her, suddenly, in the darkness on the veranda. Was it by accident, or on purpose? Evelyn did not know, but she found her cheeks flaming when she felt both his hands on her arms, supporting her, and heard his low voice:

'Oh, I say—forgive me, please!'

A rich, Irish voice. He was Irish on his mother's side. Anyone might guess that from his eyes. Blue as the lakes of Ireland, with lashes as long and black as Evelyn's own—very blue indeed in the dark tan of his rather thin face. Something about him reminded Evelyn of Gordon. His figure; his height. Gordon was tall, the same build. But somehow Gordon was flabby and this man was like tempered steel, lithe, powerful, graceful as a jungle-beast.

She smiled up at him. She could just see the blueness of his eyes in the velvet darkness of the African night; the blackness of his thick, untidy hair; the funny challenging tilt of his lips. She said:

'Oh—not at all. My fault.'

'I'm sure it was mine,' said Shane Cargill. And it was. He knew it. Hadn't he told himself last night when he saw her—slim, golden, the pale gold girl of his secret dreams—that he must meet her, speak with her, gather that gold and white loveliness to himself?

Shane Cargill had loved many women—never to his own torment. But when he set eyes upon Evelyn, a stranger unknown to him, he had recognised the fact that here was torment. Here was a new and strange desire stronger than any that had ever come upon him.

Now that he had spoken to her he could not easily let her go. With eager eyes he looked down at her, wishing he could see her more clearly. He could only smell the fragrance of her hair—unforgettable perfume. And he was glad because he had heard her speak at last and knew that her voice was cool and soft like the trickle of spring water. It was a voice which he could enjoy to hear.

'These nights are dark until the moon rises, and then they are bright and splendid,' he said.

'I am just going in,' she murmured.

'Please stay and smoke a cigarette with me and tell me I am forgiven for crashing into you so stupidly,' he said.

Evelyn found herself quite willing to do so.

9

They sat, side by side, on the veranda, and each time they inhaled their cigarettes they could see each other's faces in the red glow of the burning ends. When Shane had lit Evelyn's cigarette for her, his little finger touched hers, and a queer, electric current ran between them. Why? Who can tell? Who can solve the mystery of mutual attraction? Evelyn mused that some men mean nothing to a woman in a year and others can mean much in a moment. Such a man was Shane Cargill.

He talked to her of many things, of South Africa, of hunting, of the man's life on the veld, and of other lands he had seen and people he had met. She listened, fascinated, and wished that Gordon would talk to her like this. But Gordon had only two topics of conversation—money and food!

'How long will you be here?' asked Shane.

'I don't know,' she said, untruthfully.

'I'm glad you've come,' he said. 'The hotel was so boring, but now——'

'Isn't it still boring?' she laughed.

'No,' he said, and leaned toward her so that she could just see his lean, dark, earnest face. 'You are not like any girl I have ever met.'

'Why?' She tried not to be thrilled.

'Hasn't any man ever told you how exquisite you are?' he asked daringly.

'How silly,' she said, confused. But her pulses leaped, and she thought: 'This man has a potent charm. I ought to be angry with him for his impudence—and instead, I like him.'

'When I saw you in the lounge last night amongst that crowd of over-dressed, jewelled, exotic women, I thought you looked like a lily,' said Shane Cargill. 'You were all in white with white flowers on your shoulder. You ought always to wear white.'

The insolence of it! And he had only known her half an hour. But Evelyn was not cross. She laughed.

'You'd better design my dresses in future.'

'I'd love to,' he said. 'Would that I had the chance! Tell me more about yourself. Who are you—where do you come from, White Lily?'

'White Lily, indeed!' She gave a low laugh and he thought it was the sweetest thing he had heard —like the sweetness of the linnet's song. 'My name is Evelyn Mayton. I am generally called Eve.'

'Eve is a lovely name.'

'Yours is Shane Cargill. I like that.'

'How did you know?'

'I heard...'

That pleased him. Evelyn bit her lip, but her cheeks were dimpling. This was a rather naughty flirtation, and she ought to put an end to it. She was Gordon Veriland's future wife. But there was something irresistible about this man, and she did not want to end it.

'Tell me that you belong to yourself and to no man—Lily Girl,' said Shane. 'You aren't engaged —are you?'

Then Evelyn, with a crazy little feeling inside her, furtively slid the big yellow diamond from her marriage finger and put it in her bag.

'Do I look as though I were?' she parried.

Shane Cargill's very blue eyes half closed. He smoked in silence an instant. His heart beat furiously. She was terribly attractive, this girl with her white throat, her pale amber hair, and her cool grey eyes. He liked the gay way she responded to his flirtation. She was charming. He also believed that she was rather innocent, which made the lure

11

stronger for him. He was tired of experienced women. But his quick eye had seen that ring on her finger—and seen her slip it off.

So she was engaged, but she did not wish him to know it.

'No,' he said slowly, deliberately, 'you do not look engaged. I'm sure you are not.'

She stood up, half scared of what she was doing. 'I must go in—dress for dinner.'

'There is a dance to-night,' said Shane, standing close to her. 'May I have—every dance?'

'Of course not,' she laughed.

'We shall see,' said Shane in his rich voice, and he, too, laughed, then lifted one of her hands to his lips with a swift gesture.

'I'll be waiting for you when you come down,' he added.

He left her with her cheeks crimson and hot and her heart beating as it had never beaten before.

'I'm crazy,' she told herself.

But it was a divine madness. And this was her last week of freedom. Why not have a last fling—with Shane Cargill? He wanted an amusing, meaningless affair with her. He was the man with the reputation for breaking hearts. He wouldn't break hers. She wouldn't let him. But why not join in the game, play it with him just for fun? Once she was Gordon Veriland's wife, no more frivolity of this kind. No more admiration, no more unfettered happiness. And Shane Cargill had the bluest eyes and the brownest face she had ever seen.

'Life—you have offered me something at last,' she whispered, and stretched her hands to the rising moon. 'I'm going to take it—just for to-night—and let the world go by!'

II

The orchestra in the dance-room of the Embassy, Johannesburg, played well. Just before midnight they broke into a slow, old-fashioned waltz.

For two hours Evelyn Mayton had been dancing with Shane Cargill. He had asked for every dance —and he had had it. They had been the cynosure of all eyes. An attractive couple: the big, dark, leonine man; the slender, golden-haired girl. And because he had said she should always wear white, she was in white again to-night. A long, creamy, satiny dress with cloudy tulle to the tips of the little white satin shoes. It was cut low off the shoulders with a big bertha of delicate lace, and white roses were pinned with one diamond bar at her waist. An old-fashioned dress, but the latest thing from Paris. She was chic, exquisite, even to the white velvet coat with the huge fox collar which she carried with her because the nights in Johannesburg grow cold.

Shane Cargill's pulses had leaped when he had seen her, and there had been no other woman in the room for him from the time Evelyn entered it.

He danced well. She experienced the acme of pleasure in the curve of his steady arm. Like one in a dream she surrendered to that waltz, Noel Coward's newest one from *Private Lives*. Delicious, wistful melody. A man in the band was singing the refrain:

> 'Some day I'll find you,
> Moonlight behind you,
>   True to the dream I am dreaming.'

13

Evelyn looked up at the man who was waltzing with her. His vivid blue eyes looked down at her. And suddenly something deeper and fiercer than a mere passing attraction passed between them. Evelyn felt an almost suffocating sensation. She went very pale, as pale as her lovely dress. Shane, too, was white under his tan.

'Let's get out of this hot room,' he said.

He guided her on to the veranda, then took his arm from her. He wrapped her white velvet coat about her shoulders. They were the loveliest shoulders and arms he had ever seen—like marble in the moonlight. The exotic garden was flooded with white splendour. He was intoxicated with so much loveliness.

'Walk with me a little way,' he said.

Evelyn went with him. She thought:

'This is mad—I'm losing my head, and I mustn't. It's only a game.'

They were out of sight of the hotel now. Shane Cargill paused and took a cigarette-case from his pocket. Their eyes met in a long look. Suddenly he dropped the case on to the grass.

'No!' he whispered. 'No! I can't stand it. I must kiss you. Eve—I must. . . .'

'No, no,' she said, terrified. But her whole body was on fire—urging toward him.

'Yes,' he said. 'White Lily, the whole evening I've been crazy—haven't you known?'

She did not answer. Her hands went up to her throat, where a little pulse ached madly. She tried to remember Gordon—her fiancé—her coming marriage. But she could think of nothing but this fascinating man whose Irish blue eyes roused something in her that had been sleeping until now.

'Don't!' she whispered.

But he had taken her in his arms with a swift, fierce movement. Her pale gold head fell back against his shoulder. He took her lips like a man dying of thirst and said:

'Darling—darling—darling——'

In the white blaze of the African moonlight she stood there in his arms, crushed against him, her lips burning under endless kisses. And she knew what Life offered her to-night. Love, passion such as she had not dreamed of, and this man, Shane Cargill, as her lover, blotted out the rest of the world.

Later, strolling round the moonlit grounds with him, Evelyn knew that she ought to tell him about Gordon. And Shane knew that he ought to tell her that he *knew*. But neither of them spoke. Enchanted, like young lovers without guile, they walked—'the wickedest, nicest man in South Africa'—with his arm about her. They strolled round the gardens, only pausing now and then, when he took her wholly in his embrace.

When he bade her good-night, he said:

'I'm frightfully in love with you, darling. Do you care a little for me?'

'Yes—a lot,' was her reckless reply, and once again Gordon was forgotten—and so was that ring in her purse, and her father's crime.

'To-morrow we'll go out in my car all day and have more of this enchantment,' he said.

'Oh, let me go now, please,' she said, half afraid, wholly thrilled.

'I don't want ever to let you go,' said Shane with his lips against her throat.

She went to bed like one dazed, her lips aching from his kisses, and she thought:

'I am quite mad——'

But the 'game' went on, and Evelyn did not tell him about Gordon. Could not. She was too happy. Deliriously happy. She had not known such ecstasy existed in the world. All that next day she spent with Shane. She drove through the sunshine in his car, stopping for lunch, for tea, not returning to the Embassy until sundown. All day he was a delightful companion—and an ardent, marvellous lover. Evelyn knew that here was the man she had always wanted, and she also knew that the end of this 'game' could only be disaster. She was falling really in love—and the thing had become serious. It was no longer a game.

She wondered what he felt—what he would say if he knew. Shane was not a man to unfold his innermost thoughts, and he kept them to himself. But he found her most adorable and he told her that. And he knew that to him, this was no mere flirtation. This slender lily of a girl wielded a strange power over him. When she was in his arms and her fragrant lips responded to his kisses he was conscious of a lure more potent than he had dreamed of. He was in love with her. He wanted her. He waited for her to tell him about the other man. But while he waited he took a fierce oath that she should never belong to any man save himself.

For another day the 'game' went on, and yet another. Three mad, rapturous days with each other. And each night Shane parted from her violently reluctant. He was on fire with love for her—and she for him. It was frightful—to be parted. Evelyn could not sleep; scarcely ate; worn with longing; with depression. She loved Shane and she was going to marry Gordon. It was more than she could endure. But she had to marry Gordon—*had to*—or her father would pay the penalty of his crime. There was no getting out of it now.

'I must tell Shane,' she thought every morning before she saw him. But as soon as they were together, alone, and she felt his hands upon her, his lips on her mouth, she weakened. She surrendered to the witchery of the moment.

When he whispered:

'Sweetheart—sweetheart, do you love me?'

She answered:

'Yes, yes, with all my heart.'

How could it end save in catastrophe? Evelyn waited for the crash—for the day of Gordon Veriland's return—and knew that her heart was going to break in two when he came and she must lose Shane for always.

III

Gordon Veriland came back to Johannesburg from his mine quite unexpectedly one brilliant afternoon. He found his fiancée out. He sat on the veranda of the Embassy, drinking and waiting for her to return.

Evelyn came back just before sundown in Shane's big grey car. When she saw the tall, broad figure of her fiancé in the low cane chair, she went white as death and shrank back in the seat beside Shne.

'Oh, heavens—so it's come at last,' she thought.

She had had such a wonderful day with Shane—and she had lied, *lied* when he had asked her if she would stay with him always. She wanted to—desperately. She said 'yes'—and knew it could not be—because of Gordon. Shane put a hand over hers.

'Loveliest——' he said.

But she made no response. He followed her gaze and saw the man on the veranda, who was standing up, beckoning to her. Shane's face became grim and hard, and he removed his hand from Evelyn's.

'Good God—that's Gordon Veriland!' he exclaimed.

'You know him?' faltered Evelyn.

'Yes,' said Shane tensely. 'Do you?'

Her big grey eyes fixed themselves on his face—a face beloved to her now. Unspeakable pain wrenched her heart. But she saw the end coming and met it without flinching.

'I do. I am—his promised wife.'

The world went dark for Shane Cargill. He felt almost suffocated with rage and jealousy. She—his Lily Girl—his enchanting, adorable companion was the promised wife of Gordon Veriland. It was a frightful shock. He had known that she was engaged to somebody, but he had taken it for granted that she would break with the fellow and marry him, Shane, because of the love that had sprung so fiercely to life between them. Veriland of all men!

Two years ago Gordon Veriland and Shane Cargill had run a business together in Kimberley—connected with the mine. It was just before Shane had come into his own private money. Veriland had swindled him. And Shane, honest as daylight himself, had trusted Veriland implicitly. Veriland had been cute too. Shane had no redress when he was turned out—without a cent. But Shane had vowed to get even—to pay him back—one day.

Perhaps that day had come...

Evelyn said in a desperate little voice:

'I must—get out of the car—go to—Gordon.'

Shane's hard brown fingers closed over hers like a vice.

'Eve. Look at me.'

'No—let me go.'

'Eve—you told me you would love me for ever. Was that true?'

'Yes,' she said in a suffocated voice.

'Then you can't go to Veriland. You must explain that you have changed your mind—that you intend to marry me.'

She shivered from head to foot.

'I—can't do that.'

'Why?' he said fiercely. '*Why?*'

She shut her eyes. Oh, the agony of this! The despair! She could not tell him why—could not give her poor weak father away. She must not. She had promised to save him; to marry Gordon. She must keep her word. This affair with Shane must be wiped out utterly. And there was only one way to do it. She must lie—add another lie to the others—and in so doing, torture herself.

'Because I—prefer to marry Gordon,' she said through still pale lips.

Without a word then Shane let her go. But his eyes went dark with rage—so dark that their blueness seemed black. He stood rigid by the car, watching Evelyn join Gordon Veriland; watched Veriland take her hands, kiss her, draw her into the hotel. There was a red mist in front of Shane's eyes. He put a hand to his forehead, and it was wet.

'I can't endure this and I won't. I want Evelyn, and Veriland of all men in the world isn't going to have her,' he thought savagely.

Yes, he wanted her—madly. Had wanted her for days and nights. He almost hated her for what she had done to him. So she preferred Veriland, did she? After the way she had kissed him, after all she had said to him? By heaven, it was too much. He wasn't going to stand by and see her married to his worst enemy. He would get even with them both....

He walked into the hotel bar, his blue eyes still black with passion, and stood there drinking, thinking, making his plans.

In the hotel Evelyn faced a somewhat bad-tempered and nettled Gordon.

'Why the devil were you out with that fellow? I know Shane Cargill. Absolute rotter—not even straight in business—and can't keep his hands off a pretty girl. Damn it all, Evelyn, you're going to be my wife the day after to-morrow. A nice thing—you going out all day with a fellow like Cargill. What about the reputation of my future wife? It's beyond a joke——'

Evelyn gazed at him, distraught. She didn't believe that Shane was not straight in business. And she didn't want to hear about his affairs with other women. She loved him. Every fibre of her being ached for him. When he had left her, just now, coldly, without a word, so unlike the man who had been her ardent and adorable lover, it had been like death to her.

But she knew she dared not tell Gordon what she felt. She must placate him, calm him down, fight the horrible anguish that was in her heart for Shane, and which would be there always, day and night, from now onward.

She must remember her father—his perilous position. Gordon held him in the hollow of his hand. Her father must come first. If she were to ask Gordon for her release he would have no hesitation in landing her father in prison. He was hard—hard as nails—and she knew it.

'Don't be silly, Gordon,' she said, trying to speak lightly. 'I only went out with Mr. Cargill——'

'It's the last time such a thing is to happen, Evelyn,' he broke in angrily. 'You're going to marry me and please remember it.'

'Yes,' she said in a low voice.

He looked at her. He had forgotten how lovely she was—this slim, pale, golden girl. All the sensuousness in his nature stirred. He took her in his arms.

'Don't let's quarrel. Kiss me instead.'

She shivered and stiffened in his embrace, but she knew that she must go through with it. She raised her face to his. It was intolerable—to have to submit to this man—when she loved Shane so passionately. She looked at him with cold, critical eyes. How utterly different he was from Shane. Older; harsher. He had the same figure—he was the same height. Yet Gordon's hands felt soft—beastly—after Shane's strong magnetic fingers. When Gordon kissed her, his lips were repulsive to her—she wanted the vibrant, stirring lips of her lover, Shane.

She went down that night into the depths of depression. She did not see Shane again. It seemed that he had left the hotel. He hated her, despised her, she supposed. She would not see him again. She could hardly bear it. Yet before he came into her life she had not disliked Gordon. And many a woman in the hotel looked at her with envy tonight. Gordon was good-looking, not a grey hair. He was fair, well-groomed, had a clear complexion. His eyes were his worst feature. They were small, hazel, bad-tempered. She could well believe that Gordon would be a hard task-master and not too easy to live with unless she did what he wanted.

Evelyn was the most unhappy girl in Johannesburg that night.

IV

It was Evelyn's wedding-day. A golden, blazing South African morning. And now there was no turning back—no use to regret or despair. The bolt was shot. She had been made Gordon Veriland's wife in the Registry Office at twelve o'clock. A pale, lovely bride—paler than usual. There was no colour even in her lips. They were bright red with rouge, so nobody knew....

When she drove away from the office at Gordon's side in the big Rolls coupé in which they were to travel to Gordon's beautiful villa in the mountains, she felt almost distraught with misery. She had saved her father. She had done her duty, kept her word to Gordon.

Of course he was satisfied—full of spirits—a most ardent and attentive bridegroom. But she could not stop thinking about Shane. Oh, Shane—Shane— where was he? If only they had not separated in anger! If only he had even said 'goodbye'—'good luck'! She remembered his burning embrace, the thrill of his lips, the rich timbre of his voice, his wonderful Irish eyes. All the strength and beauty and fire of him. As his wife she would have worshipped him. Instead of which she had lost him for ever.

How could she know that he had been amongst the crowd which had gathered to see the bridal couple emerge from the Registrar's? He had seen her—watched her drive away with her husband. Mrs. Gordon Veriland—his Lily Girl—the woman he had sworn to marry.

Furious, bitter, desperate, Shane had watched and told himself that this night should not pass without retribution. Evelyn should never lie in Gordon Veriland's arms while he, Shane, was alive to prevent it.

'He swindled me, she lied to me; both of them shall pay,' said Shane Cargill.

And he had sworn that with an oath which would have made Evelyn's cheeks blanch if she had heard it.

He imagined she was content. How could he guess that all that day she suffered and dreaded the going down of the sun.

Her husband showered her with attention, with gifts. His villa was palatial, with a wonderful Italian garden; wrought-iron gateways leading into exquisite rosaries; white statues among the palms; cypresses; crystal pools full of great waxen lilies. The interior was spacious, cool, white, as luxurious as money could make it.

That night the diamond-mine owner's bride wore a necklace of jewels fit for a queen, and her slender fingers glittered with diamonds which an empress would not have disdained.

But Evelyn was conscious only of the ceaseless ache for Shane and for the might-have-been. Mechanically she smiled and talked to her husband. Cold as ice, she surrendered to his kisses when he grew amorous. But only for an instant; then somehow she eluded him. But later to-night there could be no escape. She felt that her heart would break.

They had a magnificent dinner served by two ebony Nubians, in white and scarlet uniform, in the big dining-room, which had an alabaster floor, silver walls, and scarlet-lacquered furniture. Gordon Veriland drank a lot—full of good humour and ardour for his bride. Was he not content? He had got Evelyn—his heart's desire. Now, to the devil with old Mayton in England. Let him rest in peace. Evelyn was a more precious possession than the money Mayton had done him out of.

At eleven o'clock, when the great African moon poured brilliantly down from the sky, Gordon Veriland finished a cigar and looked with a smile at his wife.

'What about turning in, pretty one?'

She swallowed hard. She was milk-white. He did not notice her pallor. She wore black velvet. He liked that. It showed off her skin and his jewels. How could he know that she had vowed never to wear white again? Shane had loved her in white, and she would wear it for no other man but him.

She moved toward the door. Gordon said:

'I'll take a last stroll in the garden and then join you, pretty one.'

She nodded and went up to her room. She hated to be called 'pretty one.' She hated everything in the world to-night, except her memory of Shane.

The bedroom was sumptuously furnished with a great golden divan against cool green walls. The long windows were open to the night, framed in green silken curtains. Here was the last word in modern furniture, and there were great masses of flowers everywhere. It was a bridal room fashioned for lovers. But Evelyn thought of Shane and wished that she could die before Gordon could come up to her and take her in his embrace.

In the garden strolled the bridegroom, smoking a last cigarette, satisfied with life and certain of happiness.

He took a walk to the garage. He had left his

gold cigarette-case on the seat in the Rolls. Better get it, in case one of those damned black niggers...

Suddenly a figure sprang upon him. Gordon gave a cry which was instantly stifled. So unexpectedly had he been attacked that his assailant, who had crept panther-like from the shadows, had the advantage and got him down on the ground without difficulty. A short sharp struggle followed, but Gordon could not call for help. A pad was pressed upon his mouth. Agile fingers tied a gag about him. Arms and legs were roped. In less than ten minutes the smiling bridegroom found himself in his own garage and in his own car—bound hand and foot, unable to move or speak. Then the doors were firmly closed and locked. Darkness and desolation descended upon Gordon Veriland, and he was left to his own furious, half-demented reflections.

Outside the garage Veriland's assailant—none other than Shane Cargill—straightened, sighed, and stretched both arms, bruised, aching from the struggle.

'God, what a business!' he thought. But he was savagely, triumphantly pleased at what he had achieved.

He walked swiftly to the villa.

There was a light in an upper-room. The rest of the villa was in darkness. That light came from Evelyn's bedroom. Shane guessed it; guessed that Evelyn was there—awaiting her bridegroom.

A grim smile played about Shane's lips.

'I could have killed Veriland,' he said—'killed him. But now, White Lily, for you——'

His very blue eyes roved to the window next to the one through which lights were shining. A dark window and balcony. That would, no doubt, be a bathroom, or Gordon Veriland's dressing-room.

There was thick foliage—some kind of tropical creeper—up the walls of the villa. Agile, graceful as a jungle creature and soundless, Shane climbed up on to the balcony and stepped softly into the room. And he found himself in Veriland's dressing-room, which had a door communicating with Evelyn's. He pushed it open. Quickly he changed, put on the white silk pyjamas and thin orange-coloured dressing-gown which were laid out on Veriland's bed.

The grim smile still played about his lips. Eve had switched out her light. So she was shy, this bride of Gordon Veriland's—shy, his Lily Girl whom he had sworn to possess. She had drawn the green silk curtains—shut out even the moonlight. All the better for his schemes. He moved slowly through the darkness.

Evelyn was standing in the centre of the room, a trembling, unhappy, white-faced little creature, shivering although the room was warm.

How she dreaded this moment—with her whole heart crying out for Shane. She felt a pair of strong hands touch her hair, then her shoulders——

She could only see the faint outline of the man in the darkness—Shane's build—Shane's height. Ah, what torture! Then she ceased to think. For the man she believed to be her husband had drawn her into his arms and she felt the pressure of his lips on hers.

V

It was grey dawn when Evelyn wakened and switched on the lights for the first time. She was surprised to find that she was alone, surprised and thankful. She did not want to face her husband yet. She lay back on the pillows and drifted into slumber again. But the name on her lips was not 'Gordon.' It was 'Shane.'

The next time she awakened it was broad daylight, and she was roused very rudely by the noise of several frantic blows on her door.

'Missus. Missus!'

It was the voice of Sambo, Gordon's valet. Evelyn rubbed her eyes, slid on her velvet wrapper, and rushed to the door.

'What is it? What has happened?'

She found half the staff gathered outside her door. Sambo's eyes rolled in his black face.

'Missus—Bwana just found—in the garage—tied up——' ejaculated the black boy.

Evelyn stared at him blankly.

'Bwana—in the *garage*?' she repeated.

'Yes, Missus, all night—must have been a robber,' said Sambo.

Evelyn put a hand to her head. It was whirling. Her face and throat were one burning blush; her body shaking. Was she crazy—or was the boy mad? There must have been some mistake.

Then she saw Gordon coming toward her; a very dishevelled, furious Gordon with a scarlet face and blazing eyes. He was rubbing his wrists. His hair stood on end. He was still in evening clothes. Evelyn gasped when she looked at him. Still in evening clothes—but how—why——?

Gordon reached her.

'My God, I'll pay someone out for this,' he shouted. 'Some swine played this dastardly trick on me. Not a cent taken off me. Not a case of robbery —just a low, filthy trick—trussing me, locking me up in my garage. Why the hell didn't you come for me—wonder where I was? You're a fine, loving bride, Evelyn.'

He raved at her—calling her names, calling his household names.

Evelyn stumbled into her bedroom. Her thoughts were chaotic, to say the least of it. But one thing stood out swamping all others. Gordon had, indeed, been the victim of some outrage and been locked in the garage. Who, then, was the man who had held her, kissed her last night? ...

The answer stood out—stabbing her heart with amazement:

SHANE! Shane Cargill—it could be no other!

Now she knew why he had not spoken once—save for a single whisper, 'Sweetheart,' against her hair. It had been Shane—Shane. He had followed. She knew it—indisputably.

'Why didn't you come for me?' Gordon bellowed at her.

Pale as a white rose, she faced him.

'Because I—I thought you had decided to—stay alone—and naturally I was not going to—to—ask you to come to me——'

Gordon Veriland smoothed back his hair. He gave a furious laugh. Then he pulled her against him.

'Little fool,' he said. 'Don't you realise yet that I'm madly in love with you?'

She felt that the last thing in the world that she wanted to do was to listen to love-making from Gordon. She had never loved him. Yesterday, after their marriage, she had realised how utterly out of sympathy they were and how impossible it would be for her to learn to care for him. She could never care for any man on earth but Shane. And now, after last night—that mad, secret hour which he had stolen so gorgeously, so recklessly—it was more than ever impossible for her to love Gordon.

She could not doubt that the man who had held her in his arms was Shane. *She knew it.* But she hardly dare let her thoughts dwell on it. Her heart seemed to stop beating at the very memory of that stolen hour. Oh, the sublime audacity of Shane! The devilment! Adorable, preposterous creature to have planned such a thing, and carried it through. Evelyn felt suffocated with the emotion of her thoughts. But she was dragged back to reality by the pressure of her husband's arms about her.

'Evelyn—haven't you a kiss for me?' he was asking. His voice was angry, resentful. 'Good God— after last night—any woman would want to make up to her husband——'

'Oh, wait—please wait!' she broke in, pushing him back from her.

'Wait for what?' Veriland frowned. 'I've waited all night tied up in a car—surely I'm entitled to one kiss from my wife. Evelyn, what the devil's the matter with you?'

She shut her eyes and warded him off with a gesture of one slim hand. Of course he could not understand. Poor old Gordon! She could almost pity him. After all, it was a humiliating and in-furiating thing to have happened to a man on his wedding night. But it was his own fault. He had forced her to marry him—bought her. In a civil-ised, polite manner he had blackmailed her into marriage—by using her father's crime as a lever.

No—she would not pity him. But herself she pitied. She felt that she would die a living death if she had to submit to Gordon after last night. She belonged to Shane, body and soul. She was his by every law. Ah, why hadn't she known *then,* while his lips had burned her eyelids and her mouth and kissed her through the silken veil of her hair, and the strong mad beat of his heart had throbbed against her breast?

'Anybody'd think you don't care a damn about me,' Gordon's voice complained bitterly, cutting through her sorrowful ecstasy of remembrance.

'Yes, yes, of course I do,' she had to say, desperately. And she told herself that she must remember her father and what danger he was in from this man. She must also not lose sight of the fact that she was legally Gordon Veriland's wife. ('Ah, Shane, Shane, reckless, mad, adorable lover, how much more am I yours,' whispered the voice of her aching heart.)

And what did Shane mean to do next? Was he going to desert her now, just steal that 'one moment in annihilation's waste'—magnificently—then go, for ever? He had done it just to shame her and hurt her and break her in pieces, because he hated her for marrying Gordon? That couldn't be. He could not mean to quit now for good and all.

Yet there was a horrible niggling fear in her mind that he might never come back. A distracting sense of loneliness and desolation filled her.

Gordon tried to take her in his arms again. She lifted a set, white face to his:

'Gordon—please—remember—I'm very upset and I—want time to think—to breathe. Besides—you—you're all dusty—dishevelled——' She tried to laugh. 'What about a nice hot bath—a change from those dinner-clothes? You look a sight!'

Gordon's arms fell to his sides. She had made him feel comic, and a man cannot be passionate when he is held up to ridicule. He reddened and eyed her in a surly way.

'Yes, I know I'm a pretty good mess for so early in the morning. I'll go along and bathe and change,' he said. 'When I come back perhaps you'll be a little more amiable. Really, Evelyn—you're very disagreeable—and we've only been married twenty-four hours.'

'Yes, I—I'm sorry you don't think me amiable,' she stammered. 'But I—everything is so upside-down, after—last night.'

'I'll damn well spend my last penny trying to find out who played that filthy trick on me,' he stormed, as he marched off to the bathroom.

Evelyn dropped limply into a chair and breathed a long sigh of relief. Thank heavens he had gone—if only for half an hour. She could be alone with her thoughts.

But they were such distracting thoughts! Half anguished—half ecstatic—they flew to Shane like homing pigeons—stayed with him—dwelt on the memory of his crazy theft of her. She stared blindly out of the long windows at the exotic gardens of Gordon's lovely villa. Sunlight shimmered over the brilliant flowers, the cool green of cypress trees, the white terraces. The sky was intensely blue. Another hot, lazy, wonderful South African day was commencing.

Where was Shane? What was *he* thinking? What would he do next?

'Supposing he does nothing—and this is the end,' Evelyn whispered to herself.

Her fair head drooped, and she pressed her closed eyelids against the curve of her arm. Her heart pounded, pounded...

'Shane, Shane, you can't desert me now,' she whispered, in an agony of terror, and tortured herself with the picture of him laughing at her and leaving South Africa this very hour.

In a short space Gordon would come back. She was his to take as he willed, his wife, his legal possession. But she could not belong to Gordon now that she was Shane's. If Shane's arms never held her again on earth, no matter. His must be the first, the last to hold her.

She sat there, brooding, worrying. The nervous colour rushed to her sweet, sensitive face when her bedroom door opened and Gordon came in again. He was in a better temper now that he had had a hot bath and changed into cool grey flannels. Self-satisfied, smiling, he approached her.

'I feel better now. It was a damned awful thing to have happened on our wedding night, but there is to-night and many other nights. My darling——'

He held out his arms. He was all passion and persuasion now. His face was flushed and self-confident. And he looked at her in a way that sent the colour from her cheeks and left her pale as drifting snow.

'Kiss me, my little wife,' he murmured. 'You must have thought me a swine not to join you last night. Poor little Evelyn!'

He was remorseful because he had not come to her last night! Evelyn felt a crazy desire to laugh. But laughter was perilously near tears. This was intolerable—she could not endure it.

He lifted her out of her chair up into his embrace.

'You look so pale, pretty one. No wonder. You lay awake wondering where I was, eh? What a fine lover you must have thought me! But I'll make up for it, now——'

Evelyn had to dig her teeth into her lower lip to kept herself from screaming. *Make up for it*—oh,

God, she didn't want him to make up for it. She wanted him to keep away—to leave her alone. What on earth would he think if he knew that instead of lying awake, wondering where he was, she had lain awake in the arms of a *man whom she had thought her husband*? Incredible, crazy adventure!

She dared not tell Gordon. That was the last thing she dared do. Not because she was afraid for herself. It was for her father she must keep quiet. Gordon had it in his power to ruin that poor, weak, lovable man who was responsible for her existence in this world.

She wondered, this morning, whether she was glad or sorry that she had ever been born.

Then, when she recalled the fierce, possessive clasp of Shane's arms, her heart leaping hotly in response, she knew that she was terribly, absurdly glad.

Gordon's lips brushed her forehead, strayed to her mouth.

'You're a sweet thing,' he whispered.

Tormented beyond endurance, she turned her head before he could touch her lips. Then—suddenly—a knock on her door. Veriland, irritated by the interruption, let her go.

'Who the hell is it?'

A servant entered; white-coated, soft-footed, deferential, with a black, shining face.

'Will the Bwana see if there is an answer to this——'

He brought Gordon a telegram on a silver salver.

Veriland, snorting, out of temper again, seized the orange envelope and ripped it open. He scanned it, then uttered a word under his breath.

'No answer. Get out!' he snarled.

The Nubian bowed and retired.

Evelyn looked at her husband questioningly.

'What is it, Gordon?'

'Everything's going wrong for me,' he said savagely, crumpling the telegram into a ball. 'Every damn thing seems to be combining to ruin my honeymoon. I've got to leave the villa at once.'

Her long lashes hid the immense relief which flashed into the clear, limpid grey of her eyes.

'Oh, Gordon—why?' She tried to infuse some regret into her voice.

'Manager of my mine has sent for me. I shall have to motor up at once. He says very urgent business that can't wait. A strike or something.'

'I—I'm sorry,' said Evelyn, and hated herself for the lie.

'With any luck I shall get back late to-night. I must,' said Veriland. 'I'm not going to be cheated of my wife like this. Good mind to take you up-country with me, only you might not stand the heat.'

'No—I'm sure I couldn't. I feel exhausted now,' she said hurriedly.

He came up to her and put an arm about her.

'You can count on me getting back,' he said in a softened tone. 'So don't look so miserable, darling. And if I don't come to-night, it will be because this damned business prevents me, and I'll get back first thing to-morrow.'

Evelyn stood dumb and rigid in the circle of his arm. She had nothing to say. She could not tell him that she did not want him back—ever. She could not disillusion him. *Dared not.* But she prayed silently that he would be prevented from coming back to-night.

She was forced to allow him to kiss her, caress her for a few moments. Then he was gone. After the big

34

car had driven away from the villa, she went to the bathroom and scrubbed her face and lips with soap and water.

'I loathe him—hate him,' she told herself. 'I belong to Shane. Oh, how can I prevent Gordon from taking me—when he comes back?'

She went into the big, luxurious sitting-room, which was a bower of flowers which shed their sweetness from great crystal bowls and delicate vases. Green sun-blinds shut out the fierce African sunlight. It was cool in here, and very lovely. Pale silver walls; jade green curtains of transparent net; a baby grand piano; a big cabinet gramophone; the latest thing in radios; the newest books from England. Every picture, rug, and piece of furniture had cost a small fortune. The whole villa was like that—costly and luxurious.

But Evelyn hated it. It was a prison to her. It was Gordon Veriland's home. Her one desire was to get away.

Her thoughts circled and revolved round the memory of last night. And now her mood changed from excitement and ecstasy to anger that slowly stirred and grew. Anger against Shane. He had had no right to do this thing to her. He had done her irreparable wrong. He had humiliated and defeated her utterly. She would never forgive, and God knew, she could never forget—even though she never saw him again in this world.

She sat down on the big sofa which was piled with great coloured cushions, jade, rose, amber, delphinium-blue, and covered with an old brocade Italian shawl of considerable worth. She covered her face with her hands and two great bitter tears stung her eyelids.

'He had no right,' she thought distractedly. 'No right——'

'*Eve!*' said a low, rich voice.

Her hands fell from her face. She sprang up—every nerve quivering in her slender body.

Shane Cargill stood in the centre of the room.

VI

Evelyn looked at Shane—as though drawn by a magnet which was irresistible. He looked back at her. Her cheeks burned to a deep rose colour. Her eyes were full of secret shame and embarrassment. But in his was a mixture of ironic amusement and of passionate appreciation.

They stared at each other—these two strange lovers—speechless for a minute. Then a gust of hot anger shook Evelyn from head to foot. She said through small, clenched teeth:

'You've come back! How *dare* you? And how *dared* you do what you did—last night?'

Shane Cargill's handsome eyes flickered.

'So you know?'

'Yes—how could I help knowing?'

'It was a good jest,' he said.

'A jest!' she repeated, blazing, indignant, 'Oh—you're unspeakable!'

'A jest that Mr. Gordon Veriland should spend the night trussed up in his own garage,' said Shane with a smile of sheer devilment.

'And that I—I——' She stopped, choking, speechless.

He came nearer her. His eyes narrowed.

'Ah! that wasn't so much of a jest,' he said very softly. 'Was it, *sweetheart*?'

Sweetheart! That name which he had breathed

against her hair in the throbbing, velvet darkness. Evelyn felt her face burn to the very roots of her blonde hair.

'You had no right. You did a terrible thing—a thing punishable by law—if you were found out——'

'But I wasn't—except by you. And are you going to give me away?'

'You deserve to be punished!'

He smiled down into her great, blazing eyes; thought how beautiful she was, and knew he could never do anything but love and desire her. But he said, in a grim voice:

'Evelyn—you, too, deserve to be punished. You fooled me. You made me love you—want you as I'd never loved or wanted a woman in my life before. I meant to marry you. I had never wanted to marry until I met you. Then you turned round on me—and married Gordon Veriland. That wasn't punishable by law, but it was culpable in the eyes of Love. So it was Love that punished you, my dear!'

She felt herself trembling violently.

'Get out—go away—don't dare stay here!' she panted distractedly.

'Oh, no,' he said calmly, and pulled a cigarette from his case and lit it. 'I went to a lot of trouble getting a pal of mine up-country to send Veriland that wire. I wanted him out of the way, and now I've got him safely at his mine I'm going to stay here and talk to you. I thought there'd be a good deal we needed to say to each other.'

Evelyn stared at him.

'*You* sent Gordon that wire?'

'Sure,' he said with his rich, lazy drawl.

'Oh—there *are* limits!' she exclaimed. But somehow anger fell from her like a cloak, and her grey eyes grew soft and brilliant with love. She loved him—adored him. He was a devil—magnificent—and the only man on earth who would ever be her lover.

'What I want—I take,' he said.

She saw his blue eyes wander from her hair to her face, to her lips, rest there. It was a look which was as passionate as a kiss. Her head seemed to spin round, and a mist blotted out the handsome, ironic face of the tall, lithe man in his cool white linen suit. She cried out, piteously:

'Shane—Shane——'

At once his cigarette was forsaken—thrown out of the window. He was at her side. She was in his arms. The one place in the world where she knew she belonged; where *he* knew she belonged. His strong brown fingers threaded through the gold of her hair, brushed it back from her face. His lips burnt against her eyelids.

'Ah, God, sweetheart—I love you so!' he said. 'I love you—love you—*love you*!'

The low, rich voice, vibrating with intense passions, brought Evelyn back from her faintness. She opened her eyes, looked up at him, and saw nothing but tenderness in the brown face that had been so cynical, so hard, just now.

'Shane,' she whispered, and burst into tears.

He held her close, close, as though he could not let her go. He drank in her tears with wild kisses.

'Hush, Sweetness—hush, Lily Girl! Don't cry. I adore you—and you mustn't cry. Darling Sweet—dry your eyes and smile at me. I love you so. Tell me you care for me.'

She was broken, defeated by love. She wound her arms about his neck.

'Yes, yes, I love you—love you, my lover!'

'You mean that?'

'Utterly.'

'You're all mine, Evelyn.'

'I know. I know.'

'Last night you didn't know.'

She trembled in his arms.

'No—last night I didn't know.'

'If you had known—would you have sent me away?'

She did not answer. But she pulled his dark head down to hers and pressed her wet cheek against the hardness of his.

'Listen,' he said, his voice rough with passion. 'If you care for me like this—why in God's name did you marry Veriland? Why? Answer me.'

She shook her head and closed her eyes. Shane saw the small pulse beating in her white throat and kissed it madly.

'Darling, darling—darling—you belong to me,' he said thickly. 'This can't go on. You can't stay here with that man. He must divorce you. If you made a mistake marrying him, and love me, then by heaven you shall come to me.'

Evelyn opened her eyes now and looked at him.

'Shane,' she said in a desperate little voice. 'You don't understand. I *can't* leave Gordon.'

'Then you're fooling me again?'

'That isn't true,' she said, and wound her arms about him feverishly. 'I love you with every drop of blood in my body.'

'Then why——?'

'Listen—I'll tell you,' she said brokenly.

She sat beside him on the sofa and the story tumbled out—with his arms holding her—his lips against her hair. And so Shane Cargill learned the truth about Evelyn's engagement to his enemy and the reason why she had lied to him and let him go out of her life.

'You see,' Evelyn finished, 'Daddy did everything for me when I was a child—he was the best of fathers—and I love him, even though he was weak and foolish. I couldn't let him down—couldn't let Gordon ruin him.'

Shane sat silent—staring into space. His blue eyes were hard stones.

'So Veriland is even more of a blackguard than I imagined,' he said. 'He robbed me once, Eve. And he has blackmailed you into marriage, tried to rob me of you. Oh, why didn't I shoot him dead last night instead of tying him up in his car?'

'Hush, my dear—don't!'

'Eve—you can't stay with him.'

'I can't leave him,' she said in a tone of despair. 'Daddy is terribly in his debt and——'

'I'm rich—I'll pay off his debts.'

Evelyn gave a twisted little smile.

'But you can't destroy those forged securities that he gave Gordon. Gordon has them in his safe in his office. I know that. He has only to use those and he can put Daddy in prison. If I leave him for you—he'll do that. He's mean and spiteful. He'll let Daddy alone if I stay with him. That's why I promised to marry him and why I must stay with him now.'

Shane stood up. His brown face was white and grim. He put a hand to his forehead.

'What a position! And you're tied to that unspeakable cad—for your father's sake? My poor Eve!'

'If I didn't love you so much it wouldn't be so hard,' she whispered. 'Shane, Shane, why did you make me care so terribly?'

He turned back to her and swept her up into his arms.

'Isn't it worth it, Sweetheart?' he asked. 'Isn't anything worth such love as this?'

She clung to him, panting, and whispered:

'Yes, yes—I wouldn't have missed it.'

'And we shall defeat this devil yet,' said Shane grimly. 'I swear that, Evelyn. You belong to me, my Sweet, and you shall never, never belong to him.'

'What shall we do?'

'I must go away and think—think things out.'

The colour left her face now. White, languid, exhausted, she lay against him, drained of vitality.

'He may come back to-night.'

'No, it's unlikely. He has a hundred miles to make, and in this heat it's very unlikely.'

'Shane, I don't want to let you go.'

'I don't want to leave you, my Sweet, but I must. I'll come again to-morrow.'

'You promise?'

'I promise—I swear it—by that wonderful hour last night, Sweetheart,' he said, and his kiss burned her lips like a flame. 'Good-bye—till to-morrow— my *own*!'

'All yours—for ever,' she whispered brokenly. She heard his car humming—heard him drive away from the villa. And she thought of the old French saying: '*Partir—c'est mourir un peu.*' '*To part is to die a little.*'

VII

Another African night fell swiftly. Starlight and moonshine replaced the burning beauty of the long day.

The luxurious villa in the mountains seemed to Evelyn the loneliest prison in the world. Shane had gone and she was utterly alone. She had only the memory of his kisses, and the now undisputable knowledge that he loved her and that she belonged to him, to comfort her.

She was worn out with the endeavour to solve this problem. How could she get away from Gordon, go to her lover, and still preserve the honour of her father?

Shane had been baffled. Evelyn was hopeless. There seemed no way out.

Sumptuous meals were served to the lady of the villa and the native servants vied with each other in the effort to wait upon her. She wanted nothing. She sat listless on the veranda after dark, brooding over the difficulties that beset her, and filled with aching longing for her lover.

Just before she went to bed a mysterious messenger brought her a note—from *him*. Something to help her through the loneliness and keep her heart from breaking.

'Sweetheart of the World—every moment, every hour is filled with the thought of you. I love you, my adorable love. I shall think of a way out. *Somehow*. I have made inquiries and hear it is impossible for G. V. to get back to-night; too far. So sleep in peace. I shall come to you again—*one night*. Good night. I worship you. Shane.'

She felt a little shiver—a flame of excitement—tingling through her. '*I shall come to you again one night*.' He said so. He loved her. Until that hour she would not live.

She learned by heart every line of this, her first

love-letter from Shane, before she burnt it for safety's sake.

She was glad that it was impossible for Gordon to get back to-night, and that she could sleep in peace.

She lay awake for a long time, staring out at the gorgeous moonlight—sleepless because of a thousand thrilling, poignant memories of twenty-four hours ago.

Later she slept soundly—because she was very tired.

She did not hear the noise of a great machine winging through the night—did not even hear footsteps on the veranda and in the villa. But she woke because somebody touched her and uttered her name.

She sat up, startled, nervous, wide awake in a moment.

'Who is it?' she gasped.

'Well, darling, I said I'd get back, and here I am,' said a satisfied voice.

Evelyn saw her husband standing beside her bed.

Dismayed, she stared at him. Instinctively her fingers reached for the swansdown wrap at the foot of her bed to put about her bare shoulders. But Veriland sat down on the bed and took the wrap away from her. He looked tired and travel-stained, but he was smiling at her eagerly. He had evidently been home some little while, for he wore pyjamas and dressing-gown.

'What a shy little wife I've got, 'pon my soul! No—let me see your lovely shoulders, darling— don't try and hide from me.'

Her heart was beating madly now with terror. Her teeth chattered.

'How did you—g-get back?'

'I flew,' said Veriland calmly. 'I was told it was

impossible for me to make the journey by car, so I got hold of an aeroplane. A Moth. Money can do anything, my dear, and I was kept from my pretty wife last night and I swore nothing should keep me from her to-night. It's just twelve o'clock. You've had a nice sleep. Did you dream of me—eh, darling?'

He took her in his arms. His lips touched her cool bare arms and her throat. Like one stunned Evelyn made no movement for a few seconds. He had flown back. She hadn't anticipated that. Neither had Shane. (Oh, Shane, Shane, if you knew—)

She passed a tongue over her dry lips. Her eyes, brilliant with fear, looked round the room as though seeking a means of escape.

'Kiss me, Evelyn,' said Gordon in a low, husky voice. 'You haven't really kissed me yet. *Kiss me*, darling.'

'No—no——' she began frantically.

'Yes,' he said, and tightened his hold of her. 'God, haven't I waited long enough for my wife? Ah! you lovely thing—don't you realise how madly I want you—all of you?'

She felt him shaking—saw the undisguised passion in his eyes, on his flushed face, and knew that Gordon Veriland, after last night's frustration, was like a madman from whom there could be no escape and to whom there could be no appeal. Her heart sank and a sick feeling came over her.

She belonged to Shane. She could not give herself to Gordon—*now*. But what in heaven's name was she going to do?

VIII

Gordon's hand was caressing her shoulder and his breath was against her cheek. Almost his lips touched her mouth. Then Evelyn sprang from the bed, seized her chiffon-velvet wrapper which lay at the foot, and covered herself with it. She could not, would not bear Gordon's embrace. White as death, shivering violently with nerves, she faced him.

He rose to his feet. He tried to look dignified and failed dismally. He cleared his throat and began:

'Really, Evelyn——'

'Please—I'm sorry,' she broke in, panting, stammering. 'I—you—oh—won't you please go to bed and leave me to sleep?'

A moment's silence. Gordon Veriland stared at her. His fingers played with nervous anger at the tassel of his satin dressing-gown. He was scarlet to the roots of his hair. He looked at his young wife's colourless face and read the dislike, the repugnance in her large eyes. Then he said between his teeth:

'So you don't want me to make love to you—eh?'

'I—you must—give me time!' she said desperately. Her heart pounded and she was thinking, in sick fear: 'Shane, Shane—what shall I do—if he won't go away?'

'Time!' repeated Gordon Veriland in a loud, angry voice. 'Good God, Evelyn—haven't we been married two days and you haven't kissed me voluntarily once—not *once*?'

She closed her eyes and put a hand on the chair near her, to support herself. Her slender body was shaking so.

'Please—I——'

'No—I'm damned if I'll go on like this,' broke in Veriland. 'You're my wife, Evelyn. You married me of your own free will. I've treated you and your father damned generously. I want my reward. I want my wife.'

She took a step backward. She looked round her in a hunted way as though searching for means of escape. She felt that she could not endure it if this man forced her into his embrace to-night. It would be wrong, a desecration—after that secret miracle of an hour—with Shane.

Veriland's anger evaporated. She looked so distractingly lovely in that pale pink velvet wrapper with delicate fronds of ostrich feather about the neck and wide sleeves. Her long, lovely neck was as graceful as a swan's; her pale gold hair curled at the nape; her eyes, brilliant with fear, glittered between the dark fringe of lashes. She was as lovely as a dream, and he had bought her, he told himself savagely. Yes, *bought* her—and he was going to have his money's worth. To the casual outsider, Gordon Veriland was a rather pompous, arrogant, conventional man. But inside he was mean, cruel, a howling cad. The cad flamed now, without reserve.

He caught Evelyn in his arms. He held her so tightly that he bruised her tender limbs and made her cry out:

'No—no—oh, please—let me go!'

'You belong to me, my dear,' he said. 'And there must be an end to this nonsense.'

Her eyes closed; exhausted with struggling, she lay limp in his arms. And she felt that she was dying—dying a slow death. She could endure mental and physical torture because she hated Gordon, and with every drop of blood in her body she loved Shane.

'It's the end—I'm lost!' she thought despairingly.

But she was wrong. A sudden crashing noise made Veriland start violently and release her. She sank on to the edge of the big divan bed, holding the back of one slender hand to her lips, and stared in front of her. Veriland also stared. That crashing noise had been a window opening wide—the windows which led on to the balcony. And through the aperture came the figure of a man in khaki riding kit—the sort of kit so many men wear in South Africa. His face was hidden by a black mask. His hands were gloved. In the right one something flashed in the electric light. An automatic. And it was levelled straight at Gordon Veriland's head.

'Hands up!' said the midnight bandit in a low whispering voice.

Veriland—always a coward and not having recovered yet from his fright after the attack upon his person in the garage last night—flung up both hands at once. He stifled an oath. Damnation! Why hadn't he a revolver on him? But he was done—in his dressing-gown—unarmed. Who the devil was this fellow? A thief—a cat burglar who had climbed up to Evelyn's window. After money, or what?

He soon knew. The burglar said—still in a theatrical whisper:

'Your jewellery.'

Veriland nodded to the dressing-table.

'In that drawer—damn you. Look here——'

'One step and I'll shoot,' came the warning.

Veriland was helpless. It was futile even to call out. The native servants were in their compound.

There was not a soul within earshot.

But Evelyn sat on the bed with every drop of blood coursing wildly through her veins and cheeks on fire. With shining eyes she regarded the 'bandit.' Veriland did not know who it was. But *she* knew. Dear God, wasn't she familiar with every line of that tall, lithe, splendid figure? Wouldn't she have known the poise, the shape of that dark, handsome head amongst a million others? Didn't she know the grim curve of that attractive mouth—the one feature not hidden by the black mask?

It was Shane. Shane had come. He had watched over her—was saving her from Gordon.

He looked at her, and she felt the very look was a burning kiss. He whispered:

'Leave this room.'

She stood up, nodded, turned and walked into the adjoining room. She did not know what he meant to do, but she fell in at once with his commands. Gordon followed the slim, beautiful figure in pink velvet with his furious eyes. What an outrage! But, of course, poor little Evelyn was scared to death of this blighter with his weapon. She had to go—to do what she was told.

'Don't move from that next room, and if you ring a bell or call a servant it will mean death to your husband,' said the bandit's mysterious, whispering voice.

Evelyn smiled to herself. What a man! The sheer devilment and cheek of it!

Shane Cargill looked at Gordon grimly through the slits of the mask. Keeping him covered, he backed to the dressing-table, found Evelyn's jewel-case, opened it, took a handful of jewels and put them in his pocket. It was necessary that he should do that to carry off this thing and prevent Gordon from guessing the truth. He would return every jewel to-morrow, by messenger.

He then concentrated upon Veriland. His swift eye sped to the bathroom—Evelyn's bathroom, which led out of this room. It had no window; there was no means of escape from it, save through this room. He ordered Veriland to get into that bathroom. Seething with impotent fury, Gordon obeyed. He was too scared of the revolver to put up any resistance. A few moments later he found himself locked into the somewhat close and scented atmosphere of his wife's bathroom. He might beat on the door and scream until dawn. Nobody would hear him.

Shane removed his mask, smiled grimly, and strolled into the next room. Evelyn was standing by the window, her slim hands pressed convulsively to her breast. She was shivering with nerves and excitement. He walked up to her and took her, without a word, into his arms.

For a long moment they clung together in a passionate kiss. He strained the slim, beautiful, velvet-clad body against him. His heart pounded madly against hers. He took his lips from hers at length and whispered against her ear:

'Darling, darling, *darling*.'

'Shane,' she panted. 'Sweetheart, thank heaven you came——'

'I was watching. I didn't trust that swine, and I wasn't going to let him touch you. You belong to me.'

'Body and soul,' she said deliriously.

'But don't you see this can't go on,' said Shane tensely. 'I can't act the bandit and get away with a hold-up like this every time.'

'I know,' she gasped. 'Shane, what can we do?'

'There must be a way out,' he said. 'We must plan something. Anyhow, I can't stay now. I must go.'

'What about—him?'

'He's safely locked in the bathroom. Keep him there. Say I've got the key and that I told you if you let him out before sunrise he'll be a dead man by sundown. That'll frighten him. He's a damned coward.'

Evelyn shivered. For a moment she strained close to her lover. His hard brown cheek was against her soft one, his lips turned to hers in another long, desperate kiss. Then he knelt swiftly and kissed her little bare feet.

'My own,' he said. 'My very own.'

He was gone—swiftly, noiselessly into the starry night—and as mysteriously as he had come.

Evelyn shivered from head to foot. What a lover! What a man! Dear life, how she loved him! She stretched both arms ecstatically above her head and shut her eyes. A long sigh came from her. He had saved her from Gordon. For to-night, at least, she was safe——

She heard Gordon's voice, yelling:

'Evelyn! Evelyn! Where are you? Come to me—let me out.'

'No,' thought Evelyn with a wry smile. 'No, my dear Gordon. I can't risk it.'

She ran to the bathroom door and told him what the 'bandit' had said.

'He terrified me, Gordon. I *know* he'll come back and shoot if I break open this door. I daren't. For your own sake, wait until morning.'

Veriland stood shivering in the bathroom. His teeth chattered. He was a frightful coward. He was beginning to be thoroughly frightened of these mysterious attacks. The first on his wedding night. Now another one, to-night. He could not conceive who the assassin was, but he realised quite definitely that he had a secret, dangerous enemy. His fury at being thwarted again, deprived once more of his beautiful wife, was swamped by his personal fear for his own skin. He remained in the bathroom all night, cursing and swearing. When daylight came, Evelyn dressed, felt safe once more, and then called for the servants, who broke open the door and let their master out.

Gordon Veriland was a pale shade of green when he breakfasted with his wife on the sunlit veranda that morning. She looked pale and heavy-eyed and languid, but there was a tinge of amusement in her eyes which he did not notice. He raved violently all during the meal. He was going to put the matter in the hands of the police. He would have the villa watched; he would have a personal bodyguard. He would find this infernal criminal or die in the attempt. A lot of talk, bravado, to which Evelyn listened with cool scorn. But her heart sank a little. If Veriland kept his word and had the villa watched, it would certainly mean that Shane could not come again. She would not be saved from Gordon's embrace a third time.

'Thousands of pounds' worth of jewellery that I've given you were taken last night,' Gordon raged. 'And do you know, Evelyn, when I got to my mine, I found I had been *tricked* there?'

Evelyn cheeks coloured, but she kept her gaze on her plate.

'Really?' she murmured.

'Yes. My manager hadn't sent that wire at all. There's some devil's work afoot. Look here, we'll leave this villa. The damned place is haunted.

We'll go off to the coast somewhere. I'm not going to be kept away from my wife to-night, I swear it.'

But Gordon Veriland was not allowed to keep that oath, much to Evelyn's relief. A telephone call came through from the mine during breakfast—from his manager, Mr. Davidson, and this time Gordon knew it was no bogus message. He spoke to Davidson personally. Something very important had happened at the mine. A strike—the miners wanted higher wages. Mr. Davidson was worried, and advised that Mr. Veriland should come at once to settle the dispute. The attitude of the miners was rather nasty, and Davidson would not answer for the safety of the mines and offices unless Mr. Veriland came immediately.

Gordon Veriland had sworn to hold his wife in his arms to-night, but he was more concerned about his personal safety and his money, all of which came from his mine, than he was about passion. Aggravating though it was, he must go at once up-country. At least he would be free, there, from these terrifying attacks made upon him by masked robbers. He was almost relieved that Davidson sent for him.

Evelyn was a good deal more relieved when she heard the news, though she tried not to appear so. Veriland put an arm about her and scowled at her charming, beautiful face.

'I'm damned if I like leaving you here. Hadn't you better come along?'

'I'm not frightened at being left—I never was nervous—and I'll have two of the boys to sleep on the veranda at nights,' she said quickly. 'I can't come with you, Gordon. Haven't you said, yourself, it's frightfully hot up-country and that I couldn't stand the rough life—the discomforts there?'

'Yes, that's true,' he muttered.

'You won't be away long, will you?' she said.

'One never knows—when these strikes and disturbances start. Davidson has no authority with the men—I can manage them—I may have to stay up there a bit,' said Veriland in his boastful fashion. 'It will mean a big loss of money to me if the mine's closed down. But I'll get back as soon as I can, and then, darling'—he drew her close—'our honeymoon must begin—at last!'

Evelyn did not answer. Her face was hidden against his shoulder. But she thought of Shane, and told herself that never, never while she could prevent it should that 'honeymoon' with Gordon ever take place.

IX

Evelyn was alone for a very short while after Gordon drove away from his villa. Soon after lunch Shane came. Not Shane, the masked bandit, but Shane Cargill, the well-dressed, debonair man whom she knew and adored. Their relief and joy at being together was unbounded. They spent a feverish hour in the cool, beautiful drawing-room, sitting side by side on the sofa with their arms about each other.

'What luck—what colossal luck—getting a genuine call from the mine,' said Shane. 'I was beginning to wonder how the devil to protect you again to-night, Loveliest!'

She said, with her cheek pressed to his:

'It *is* lucky—and Gordon was such a hopeless coward that he was glad to get away after last night.'

'Sweetheart,' said Shane, looking down into her

sparkling eyes. 'Do you realise what this means?'

'Yes,' she whispered. 'That we can be together as much as we want and that there isn't a soul on earth to prevent our meeting.'

'Yes,' he said. His arms tightened about her. 'I can stay with you most of the day. We'll go out together in my car—drive up the mountains—down to the lakes—have glorious, lovely picnics like we used to have.'

'Only much better, Shane, because we love each other so much more.'

'I shall have to leave you at night-time, but not until the last possible moment,' he murmured.

Her slim hands drew the dark, handsome head down to her fair one.

'Shane, Shane, if only we need not separate.'

'One day we won't have to, beloved.'

'I'd go to the ends of the earth with you,' she said ardently. 'You know that. But I daren't leave Gordon because of poor Daddy.'

'I understand, Sweetheart.'

'Never mind—let's forget everything except that we can be together now—for many lovely hours.'

He looked at her through half-closed eyes, his pulses leaping hotly at the beauty of her. She was wearing one of her loveliest dresses—a long white chiffon dress with little red printed flowers and a red belt. It clung to the supple lines of her exquisite figure. There were big red beads twisted about her pale throat like huge translucent rubies, and red flowers on her shoulder. She leaned back on the cushions, smiling at him divinely. His arms went round her and his lips strayed to her eyes, sealing them with kisses.

'Adorable!' he said fiercely between the long kisses. 'Dear Adorable! It wasn't fair that you should be sacrificed to that rotten coward—it wasn't fair. You and I were made for each other. I have no compunction in taking you. You belong to me.'

'Utterly,' said Evelyn.

The liquid gold of the sunshine filtered through drawn silk curtains and green shutters and bathed her in a warm glow. The South African afternoon was hot and drowsy, and the natives slept and lazed in their compound. There was not a soul to see, to care. Evelyn and her lover, locked in each other's arms, lived those golden, feverish hours to the full—lived madly each for the other.

When it was sundown, Evelyn changed into a chiffon evening gown of sweet-pea pink—a colour that matched her delicately flushed cheeks. Shane thought her adorable in it. He took her in his car to a hotel in the mountains; they dined on the terrace in the starlight with a rosy lamp on their table, and an orchestra playing softly as an accompaniment to all the wonderful things they had to say to each other.

It was a perfect evening for them both. It ended on a joyous note, for when Shane took Evelyn back to her villa, they found a telegram waiting from Gordon Veriland. A long, grumbling wire. Things were much worse at the Jeeburg mine than he had anticipated. Davidson, his manager, had gone down with fever. It looked as though Gordon would have to stay up-country for several days—if not several weeks.

Evelyn read this telegram, and then looked at Shane with starry eyes.

'That means we can be together lots and lots. Oh, Shane, my dear!'

'My Sweet!' he said. 'The fates are kind.'

He took her silver cloak gently from her, stooped and kissed each dimpled shoulder in turn. He took the lovely young figure in the delicate pink dress into his arms and kissed her madly on lips and throat.

'If only I hadn't to leave you—but I must,' he said huskily. 'There are the servants to cope with, and I can't possibly stay. But before I go—tell me again that you are all mine, Eve, my heart!'

She told him speechlessly, with lips and straining arms and the mad, sweet throb of her heart under his own.

But after Shane had gone, she lay sleepless, troubled, telling herself that this dream of passion, of ecstatic happiness, could not go on. How could it end? Was she very wicked? Was this love a sin? In the eyes of the law, yes. But she had been forced, for her father's sake, into marriage with Gordon. By every law of love she belonged to Shane. It was too utterly cruel to contemplate that she dared not go away with her lover and legalise their love; dared not, because of what Gordon knew about her father.

There was nothing to do but to live for the passionate present and hope that something would happen to make everything come right.

So the days passed. Evelyn and Shane were scarcely out of each other's company. They spent the long, golden African days together and parted only late at night when he was forced to leave her.

Never for an instant did their passion wane. The more Evelyn saw of Shane the more she admired him, his wonderful good looks; his humour; his gay, charming personality. The more the man saw of her, the more he loved her. She was so absolutely unspoiled and sweet. As lovers they were a perfect pair.

But how could it end? Only in disaster. In their hearts both of them knew that, feared it; and put off the evil day of reckoning.

A month—six weeks—two months passed. Gordon Veriland did not come back. He wrote constantly—long, complaining letters. Davidson's fever had turned to pneumonia. He had been desperately ill in hospital up-country and nearly died, and was only just regaining health. Veriland dared not leave the mine because, although the men were pacified and back at work, they were on edge and needed coaxing and managing. Veriland was training a young Englishman to take Davidson's place. He could not get back. When he did get back, he wrote to Evelyn, they would go right away—leave Africa—travel a bit together and have that 'long-deferred honeymoon.'

The very words made Evelyn shudder. All these days and weeks she and Shane had been together, and she was so much more his than ever, now. How could she possibly give herself to Gordon and *live*? she asked herself.

She told Shane what her husband had written. Shane's very blue eyes looked grim.

'It must be prevented, my Sweet,' he said.

'But how—how?' she cried in despair on that day that Gordon's letter came. A day shadowed for them both, and even while Evelyn lay in her lover's arms the memory of Gordon and the threatened 'honeymoon' haunted her and spoiled the thrill of Shane's kisses.

But nothing could spoil the divine thrill of those burning kisses for long. Evelyn lived from day to day, from night to night, in an ecstatic dream—an ardent, secret, lovely dream shared with her lover. When he was with her nothing on earth mattered. She could not tire of his arms, his caresses, and Shane, who had been so devil-may-care, so indolent about his love-affairs until he met Evelyn, lived only for the hours when he was with her. He was restless, impatient, crazy to get back to her side as soon as he left her.

They loved to dance together. All her life, Evelyn remembered one night, about a fortnight after Gordon's letter had temporarily destroyed her happiness, when she dined with her lover in his bungalow, and they danced to the tune of an electrically-run gramophone on the veranda in the brilliant African moonlight.

Shane had rented this bungalow especially to be near Evelyn. An expensive, luxurious little place built high in the mountains, which belonged to a South African millionaire who was in Europe at the moment.

There, in Shane's home, Evelyn was happier than she could ever be in Gordon's magnificent villa. Long after the servants had gone to the compound for the night, they danced, these two who loved each other so madly, out there on the veranda where the air was sweet and cool and only the stars and the great white moon could witness their happiness.

An unforgettable night for Shane, as well as for the woman he loved. He put on a waltz record, the latest from England, the plaintive, lilting melody from *Bitter-Sweet*.

Through the open french windows came the soft refrain; amber lamp-light—falling gently upon Evelyn; a golden girl in a long chiffon dress of palest gold to match her hair. Shane held her in what he laughingly told her was 'quite the wrong way'—both arms about her slim waist as they moved in perfect unison up and down the veranda.

> *'I'll see you again,*
> *When spring breaks through again.'*

She sang the words softly, reaching her sweet red mouth up to his ear. He waltzed with her, the blood coursing madly through his veins, and whispered back:

'My Sweet, my darling—before spring—long, long before that I must see you again. I love you so!'

'I love you, Shane—but it's late—I must go home.'

'Don't say that. Your home is here, with me.'

'It ought to be—by every right. But fate's unbelievably cruel to lovers. I must go—back—anyhow.'

'Yes, and I must take you. Oh, darling!'

His lips met hers; clung in a dizzying kiss. They waltzed on in that close embrace—Evelyn felt that he drew her very heart from her body in that mad, lovely dance.

Then suddenly she felt a queer pain in her head—a sudden giddiness. She went very white, and he felt her grow limp in his arms.

He stopped and looked with concern down at her pale face—a rapt, bewildered face, with closed eyes.

'Darling—what is it?'

'Shane—Shane—I—don't know. But I feel—ill—queer. You must take me back.'

He was at once frantic with worry about her. He put her coat about her beautiful bare shoulders;

carried her into the bungalow; laid her on his sofa and knelt beside her.

'You can't go back till you're better, my Sweet. What is it? How pale you are—and you're trembling.'

She lifted her long lashes and looked at him. For a while she did not speak, but she took his hand and drew it up to her lips and held it there, breathing spasmodically. Her heart seemed to be going at a frightful rate, and she still felt giddy—strange. A terrific, overwhelming thought had flashed into her mind. A thought that had been there for the last week, but she had scarcely dared foster it or breathe it to Shane. Indeed, she had not allowed herself to dwell upon it.

But now it came back and assumed tremendous and vital importance. Pressing Shane's warm brown hand against her lips she lay on the cushions in his room and *knew*—knew indisputably what had happened to her—why she had so nearly fainted during that dance just now.

Big-eyed, white with emotion, she whispered her lover's name.

'Shane!'

'My Sweet—what is it? Tell me!' he said.

'Shane—something terrific—has happened to me —something we did not think of. Oh, God, how mad we've been—and yet how glad I am, in a way——'

He caught her close and looked down into her eyes earnestly. His heart seemed to stop beating, and he, too, went white.

'Evelyn—you don't mean—*that*!'

She clung to him, half terrified, wholly enraptured.

'Shane, I'm going to have a child—your child.'

Shane Cargill was dumb for a moment and into his handsome eyes leapt fear—not for himself—but for her.

'Eve—Sweetheart—are you sure?'

'Yes—to-night—I am sure.'

'What have I done?' he said hoarsely. He leaned his dark head against the yellow chiffons on her breast. 'I ought to be murdered for this. You—a mother—of my child. *Evelyn!*'

She put her arms about him, held him close, covered his head with kisses, and the tears rained down her cheeks.

'I love you so, Shane. I want your son. I'd love it more than anything on earth. But what will Gordon do to Daddy out of revenge when he finds out? Shane, he'll know it can't be his, because I've never lived with him.'

'I know,' said Shane, tight-lipped. 'It's the very devil, darling. I had no right——'

'Hush,' she broke in. 'I love you. I'm more than ever yours now, my dearest.'

'Utterly mine. You—and my child. Oh, my darling!'

He drank her tears away with his kisses; smoothed the fair, bright hair back from her hot forehead; kissed her hands from finger to wrist. He adored her—and this thing which might have been so wonderful, so beautiful, filled him with fear for her sake.

'God knows what we can do now,' he said. 'I must think. There's Gordon Veriland to be reckoned with. I want to take you right away now, but I can't because of your father. It's a hideous position. And you—such a child yourself, to bear my child. Oh, Sweetheart—forgive me!'

'I'm not afraid of that—there's nothing to forgive. I only want to prevent complete chaos,' she whispered brokenly.

Much later he took her home. He could hardly bear to leave her. He came to her bungalow first thing next morning. She had seen a doctor. She knew now there was no mistake. She alternated between rapture and terror of the future—and the one overwhelming, tormenting question which she asked herself was: 'How can I live without Shane now—now that I am to give him a son?'

The knowledge enthralled and terrified her, both. To bear Shane a son—blue-eyed, black-haired, devil and saint combined, adorable and captivating—like *him*—what heaven! But under the present conditions heaven might be hell.

All that day he stayed with her, exquisitely gentle and tender with her; adorable, she thought; worrying if she showed the slightest sign that she was weary; pouring his devotion, his love upon her. She was not only the woman he loved and desired; she was the mother of his child, and he was aching with love for her but grimly aware of the disaster of this thing—the difficulty of their position.

Unknown to them, meanwhile, during that long hot day, Gordon Veriland was being driven in his powerful car down from the Jeeburg mine toward his villa. He had settled the miners' dispute finally and installed a new manager. He was eager and impatient to be home. But he was not going to Evelyn in any too amiable a temper. He was ridden with jealousy. Rumour had reached him, up-country gossip—spread in the first instance by one of his own native servants—that his young wife was consoling herself in his absence. With whom Veriland did not know. He had merely heard that a man was constantly at the villa and that Evelyn was out with him most of the day and half the evening.

Gordon Veriland—brooding over this as he journeyed homewards, vowed vengeance on the man, whoever he was. He was not going to let Evelyn play any game like that with him. She had married him and he was her master; the man to whom both she and her father owed a heavy debt. It was a debt she was going to pay, he told himself grimly. If she was fooling round with other men he would make her pay doubly dear.

He had a new automatic in his coat-pocket. In future he did not intend to be without it. He was too afraid of further mysterious attacks from masked robbers, once he was back in his mountain villa.

He thought of Evelyn's seductive beauty, and passionate jealousy flamed in him. Every mile that he covered, he thought:

'Another mile nearer her, and to-night, my wife shall be made to realise that she *is* my wife. Perhaps there's no real truth in this damned rumour about her and this fellow. But if there is, she'll answer to me for it—as she'll see.'

He had deliberately refrained from warning Evelyn of his return home to-night. He would surprise her; just walk in and see what she was doing.

He grew cunning and more suspicious as the day deepened into night. When he came within a quarter of a mile of his villa he told the native chauffeur to stop.

'I'll walk these few yards,' he said. 'You stay here and then drive up in half an hour's time with my luggage.'

The chauffeur saluted. It seemed a strange request, but the Bwana was strange at times.

Gordon Veriland, like a big, stealthy jungle

animal, padded through the still starry night, and made his way noiselessly to his villa.

He saw one light shining from the drawing-room. Evelyn was there. Was she alone? He would soon see—test her fidelity for himself.

A nasty smile played about his lips. He fingered the automatic in his coat pocket. Without making a sound he stepped on to the veranda and saw that the windows were wide open to the lovely night, but the silken curtains drawn. He pulled one of the curtains gingerly apart.

Then his face went livid and his eyes black with rage.

So the rumour was not without very good foundation. Evelyn was consoling herself and very happily. She lay on the sofa against a pile of gold cushions; lovely, languid, in a white lace negligée. Kneeling beside her, his arms about her, his back turned to the window, was a tall, dark-haired man in evening dress.

Instinct warned Evelyn. Her startled gaze sped to the window—she saw her husband's livid face and cried out.

Her lover turned his head swiftly. And then Veriland saw and recognised him as his old enemy —Shane Cargill. It was Shane, kneeling there, with Evelyn in his arms—Shane Cargill who was obviously her lover.

Gordon Veriland went mad with rage.

Cargill, his old enemy, was Evelyn's lover. So it was true—Evelyn *was* unfaithful to him. The rumours were well-founded. Such revelation was bad enough, but the fact that Shane Cargill was the man in the case made things doubly worse in Veriland's eyes. He had done Shane a wrong; he knew it. So he hated him. A human being so often hates and resents the one he has injured.

Evelyn screamed again—hoarsely—frantically.

'Damn you to hell, Cargill,' said Gordon, and sprang, pulling the automatic from his pocket.

But Shane was on his feet now—ready for him. He too sprang. They met and grappled, furiously, with bared teeth and panting breath—primitive, all shackles of civilisation flung off—two male creatures fighting for possession of a woman.

Evelyn managed, somehow, to gain her feet, but she trembled so that she could scarcely stand. The shock of her husband's sudden and unexpected return was so great that it told on her whole nervous system. She was not in a fit condition to cope with it, and she could make no physical effort to stop them fighting—no matter how much she wanted to. She tried to take a step forward and pull at Shane's arm. She could not move. Deathly white, she watched, one hand against her lips.

'Oh, don't, don't, *don't*!' she kept on gasping.

The two men took no notice of her; Gordon Veriland was in an insane rage and Shane was a match for him. Veriland's chief emotion was jealousy—furious jealousy because he had seen his beautiful, attractive wife in the arms of a man who was obviously her lover. And never had that lovely body yielded to *his* kisses so willingly; never had her arms been curved about *his* throat so generously.

'Damn you, Cargill!' he said again, sobbing with rage.

In Shane the devil was unloosed; a grim torrent of fury against this man who had forced Evelyn to marry him—using her father as a lever. Not only had he done Evelyn a wrong, but he had betrayed him, Shane, in the past. His fingers itched to get at

65

the traitor's throat. He had no weapon, and he saw the revolver glittering in Veriland's hand. But he fought magnificently and unafraid. They were much of the same height, and although Shane was lither, more muscular, they were well-matched during that battle. Gordon, being flabbier, stood less chance as the moments ticked by. He breathed stertorously; his face and neck grew scarlet, his eyes protruded. Shane almost had him down that time. Shane—his blue eyes like tempered steel in his brown face—suddenly laughed.

'A fight to the finish, Veriland,' he panted. 'And Evelyn belongs to—the victor—eh?'

'Oh, Shane—Gordon—stop, for God's sake,' said Evelyn's moaning voice.

She could not bear this fight between the man she loved so terribly and the man to whom she legally belonged. That automatic was still between Gordon's clenched fingers. If it went off—if Shane got hurt...

Gordon felt a sudden dizziness in the head. He was a coward, and the rage which had given him courage was dying down. He began to be afraid that Shane would have him down and out. And so he did a low, cowardly trick.

'Look out, man—Evelyn's fainting,' he gasped.

Shane loosened his grip and swung round, all concern for Evelyn. He heard her shriek:

'He'll shoot you—*mind*!'

Then there was a report and a horrible, sickening pain in Shane's shoulder. A red mist blotted out Evelyn's terrified face. He dropped soundlessly at her feet.

Veriland had shot him in the back.

Evelyn looked at her husband in horror and loathing.

'You coward—you filthy coward—to shoot him when his back was turned—when he had no weapon—oh, my God—you coward!'

Gordon Veriland pocketed the smoking automatic. He felt sick and afraid of what he had done, but relieved that he was personally out of danger. He stepped across Shane's prostrate body and caught his wife in his arms.

'Damn you and your lover,' he said between his teeth. 'If I shot him, he deserved it—and you——'

She heard no more. The room was turning upside down. Through a mist of agony she saw Shane's dark, beloved head on the carpet—his face hidden from her—his body terribly still. She believed that Gordon had killed him. Murdered him—her lover—the father of her coming child.

She fainted dead away in Gordon's arms.

Gordon Veriland was not sorry. Evelyn, unconscious, would be easier to deal with. Jealous rage had cooled in him. He felt uneasy and anxious to get away from the sight of his victim's body. He picked Evelyn right up and carried her out of the room. Holding her thus, helpless, soft, so delicately lovely, against him, he thought:

'She's my wife, and to hell with her lover or what has happened. She's going to belong to me now.'

He carried her to her bed. Her faint was a deep one, and she made no movement. Veriland returned to the drawing-room and knelt down beside Shane. He turned him gingerly over and grimaced when he saw the blood oozing from the round black hole which the bullet had made in his shoulder. But he saw at once that Shane was not dead. He was breathing. Gordon Veriland was glad of that. He had no wish to hang for murder, otherwise, so far as his feelings were concerned, he would have been only too pleased to see Shane dead at his feet.

He hurried on to the veranda and rapped out orders to his chauffeur.

'There has been an accident—the Bwana must be taken to his own bungalow. Find out from the other boys where he is living. I see his own car is there. Take it and drive the Bwana home, then get him a doctor.'

The chauffeur saluted.

'Yes, Bwana.'

Five minutes later, Shane, still breathing, but bleeding profusely, was roughly bandaged and driven in his own car back to his own home.

Veriland breathed a sigh of relief and returned to his wife.

Evelyn's eyes were open now; eyes wide and big with the horror of remembrance. She sat up in bed, panting, a hand to her throat, and stared at Gordon.

'Ah—you—*killed* him!'

Veriland looked down at her through half-shut eyes. Then a slow, cruel smile curved his lips.

'Yes,' he said deliberately. 'You are right, Evelyn. I—killed him.'

'He's dead?'

'Yes. Damn him—he's dead. His body has been taken to his own place.'

Silence. Evelyn's heart seemed to beat at a furious rate, then failed her. She lay back on the pillows, white, exhausted, drenched with perspiration. Her golden hair clung damply to her forehead, and into her large eyes came a look of such agony, such despair, that Gordon Veriland turned from her uneasily. Did she care for the fellow as much as that? Perhaps he ought to tell her Shane lived. No—be damned if he would. Evelyn belonged to him and had treated him deuced badly. Let her imagine the fellow had passed out. Tomorrow he would take her away and begin again. He wasn't going to lose her. He wasn't going to be cheated of his rights any more.

He sat down on the edge of the bed and took her hand. It was limp, nerveless, ice-cold. She made no attempt to withdraw it. She was broken with anguish because Shane was dead—Shane whom she loved better than anything, anybody on earth—too broken to make resistance of any kind. Speechless, she lay there and looked blindly beyond Gordon out at the African moonlight.

An hour ago she had been so happy—in Shane's arms. His warm, ardent lips, his strangely thrilling hands, caressing her, had blotted out the rest of the world for her. And now, chaos—tragedy—death. Shane was dead—shot—murdered in a brutal, cowardly fashion by this man who had come back like the stealthy, vile coward that he was.

The fact hammered in her brain until she felt she would go mad. Shane was dead. *Shane—dead*. That fine, lithe, graceful, powerful body, so full of youth and vitality and strength, was still—rigid—cold—never to move again. Those sensitive, sun-browned fingers which had so often held her and played with her hair were stiff and would never touch her again. Those gay, reckless, handsome blue eyes were filmed and closed in the final long sleep.

'No, no, no!' said Evelyn suddenly, in a frantic voice. ''I can't *bear* it!'

Gordon Veriland cleared his throat.

'Listen to me, Evelyn, you're my wife and you owe me an explanation. How long has Cargill been your lover?'

She wrenched her hands from him now.

'Don't touch me—don't speak to me—I hate you—despise you!'

'Wait a moment,' he said harshly. 'That's all very well. You've been fooling round with this man in my absence and you're married to me. What about your father? I've been fooled and cheated enough. Any more nonsense about hating me and crying for your lover, and your father can go to prison. D'you see?'

She opened her lips to speak, then shut them again. Her momentary flame of resentment, of wild hatred of this man, passed. Despair settled over her again. She still had her father to think of, and Gordon was relentless.

Besides, Shane was dead, so what did anything matter now? Yes, something mattered—something was left. Her child. *His* child.

The thought of her baby—flesh and blood of that idolised lover—came sweeping back into her numbed and suffering mind and drowned all other thoughts. She grew calm and contemplative. She must be calm—for her baby's sake. And she must use cunning, too. Whatever happened now, Gordon must not know that she was bearing Shane's child. He must think it his for all their sakes. Only in that way would it be possible for her to bring the child so passionately desired into the world and bring him up in peace. No use now to tell Gordon the bitter truth and risk him throwing her father into prison and heaping shame and scandal upon her and her baby.

'Shane, Shane, my darling, you've left me for ever—and now I must do my best for your son,' she thought, her tears falling thick and fast. 'Nothing else matters. I don't matter—let Gordon do what he wants, now.'

She suddenly put out a hand and spoke to her husband in a broken voice:

'Gordon—you may think I have wronged you—but I think you wronged me even more when you made me marry you to save my father. We are quits. Very well. Shane Cargill is out of it'—she swallowed hard and continued with a mighty effort: 'Let us forget it—go away—start again.'

Veriland leaned over her eagerly.

'You mean that? By heaven! if you'll be nice to me, Evelyn, I'll forgive this lapse of yours and you shall have all that money can buy—darling——'

He put his arms about her. She shuddered and thought:

'What money can buy—oh, heaven! but I only want what money cannot buy—my lover—Shane back again—my Shane.'

She looked at Gordon piteously.

'Will you leave me alone to-night—please—and give me a chance to get over this? I feel—so unnerved.'

He was eager to snatch her now into his embrace, but he had the decency to grant that request.

'Yes, very well. Go to sleep. To-morrow, very early, please be ready to leave here. I want to get away before Cargill's death becomes public news.'

He left her. She lay motionless, suffering terribly, and wishing that the bullet which had killed Shane had entered her heart as well. But she must live—for their child. And there was hell to be faced before that child came. Perhaps it was punishment for the sweet, secret sin she had shared with her lover. She did not know. She only knew that all her life she would go on remembering every moment they had spent together, and that she would want him, madly, hopelessly, *terribly*, until she died.

X

The next two days and two nights were dreadful and unforgettable for Evelyn. She was so stunned with the horror of Shane's death that she did anything and everything that her husband asked of her.

Those two days and nights were spent in travelling—which at least meant that she was spared from Gordon's love-making. But he never left her side, and he showed continually that he was her 'lord and master,' and that when this journey ended she must be made to realise the fact.

Soon after sunrise, following the terrible night of the shooting of Shane, Evelyn and Gordon left the mountain villa by car. Her things were hastily packed and by midday she found herself in the train bound for the coast. Gordon took her right the other side of South Africa—a forty-eight-hour journey—to a small, exquisite place on the bluest of blue seas, where there was one big hotel. A luxurious retreat for millionaires who wanted relief from burning suns and the parched plains. Here it was cooler than in most places—the white hotel, its balconies festooned with climbing flowers, was built on the beach, and at the back lay a glorious garden of palm trees and fruit and flowers.

Gordon ushered his young wife into their magnificent suite which overlooked the shining sea, and said:

'Here we will at last begin our real honeymoon.'

She did not answer. Her eyes—big and tragic, in

a face grown white and too thin—looked beyond him to the sparkling, sunlit water. A beautiful spot, this Jalessa—one of the chosen spots, for lovers, in South Africa. For lovers—ah! she wanted to forget that word and all that it implied. Hundreds of miles away her lover lay dead. Perhaps to-day he was being buried.

Gordon had brought her here for a *honeymoon*.

How could she bear it? She was inclined to rush out on to the balcony and fling herself on to the rocks below—end all the grief and torment of remembrance—especially the memory of Shane's stricken eyes when he had fallen at her feet. But she must not do that. There was always the child to be thought of. Poor little thing. What a beginning to its life! She sat down wearily on the edge of the bed as the coloured servants carried in the luggage. Gordon, smoking a cigarette, walked up and down with a pleased look on his face.

'We'll be very happy here and wipe out the past completely,' he said.

Still she made no answer. But she closed her tired eyes. Gordon had never asked for details of her affair with Shane. They had agreed to 'wipe it out.' And never once had he suspected her condition. No—he did not know about Shane's child. So it must come into this world as his. The thought of what lay in store for her nearly broke her heart. To give herself to Gordon now—after she had belonged to Shane—ah! that was the bitterness of death itself. A death she must needs die for the sake of the baby—and her father.

Gordon Veriland, trying not to notice his young wife's tragic expression, felt quite pleased with everything. There was a wire in his pocket now, from a trusted servant left up in the mountains, assuring him that Shane Cargill lived, so that he had not got murder on his soul. He was in excellent spirits all that day.

He dined with Evelyn on the terrace beside the sea, under a starlit sky, and drunk a toast.

'To our new life—which begins to-night.'

She tried to smile, but the tears scorched her eyes, and she could not raise her goblet in answer to that. But she thought:

'I must go through with it—for my baby's sake.'

She had never looked lovelier than that night in her black chiffon gown. Like a pale lily with her golden hair and snowy arms and throat, with lilac shadows under her eyes. Gordon Veriland knew no pity—only desire—whenever he looked at her. She was his wife and he had been cheated twice of her. But never again.

Later that night, while she stood at her bedroom window, in her velvet wrapper, waiting for Gordon to come up to her, Evelyn stared blindly at the moonlit sea and whispered:

'Shane—Shane—my darling—this time you can't save me and I mustn't spare myself. But I wonder how can I endure it?'

Gordon walked into the room, eager, smiling, quite handsome to-night, and in his most amiable mood. But Evelyn looked at him with hatred and loathing. The man who had murdered Shane—ruined her and the father——

He took her in his arms.

'My wife,' he said. 'Kiss me.'

She shut her eyes and trembled. She thought:

'Shane, Shane—forgive me—darling—it's for our child's sake.'

That first night in Jalessa, the flower-filled African paradise on the sea, Evelyn went down to the very depths of mental suffering, of despair.

But away in the mountains, in the days that followed, Shane Cargill, by no means dead, experienced a hell of his own. The wound which had been inflicted by Veriland's revolver was only a flesh one, and Shane, being perfectly healthy, recovered swiftly. His shoulder was healed in less than a month.

His first frantic worry was about Evelyn. As soon as he could get over he drove up to her villa, but only to find it shut up, and nobody could tell him where she had gone; neither could he discover from any inquiries what had happened to Gordon Veriland. The Verilands had just vanished mysteriously from everybody's ken.

Shane nearly went mad. Of course, he saw it—Veriland had taken Evelyn away, and she had had to go with him—because of her father. He had lost her—her and their child. The idea that Gordon now possessed all that had been his and so utterly dear to him nearly robbed Shane Cargill of reason. What he suffered from the wound in his shoulder was nothing. But he went through a purgatory of mental anxiety and misery.

He did not know how to face life without Evelyn. But he had no redress, no hope. If it had not been for her father and that dangerous knowledge which Veriland possessed, Shane would have searched Africa for her and then taken her away to the other side of the world. Her and their child. But his hands were tied.

There was a grimmer, tighter twist than ever to Shane's lips when he was quite well and about again. He went back to Johannesburg and hung round—lonely—unhappy—aching for news of Evelyn—hoping to discover where she had gone.

He felt that he must see her again, if only once, and make sure that she was all right.

It was at a bar, drinking with a crowd of other men in an hotel in Johannesburg, that the first news of Evelyn came to Shane. Weary, indifferent to what was going on round him, his handsome eyes darkly brooding, Shane suddenly sprang to attention. He heard the name 'Veriland.' He swung round to the man who had mentioned it, an elderly South African, interested, like Gordon, in diamond mines.

'Do you happen to know where Veriland is these days?' asked Shane, every nerve jumping.

'Yes—I came across a fellow who'd run into him at Jalessa.'

'Jalessa!' repeated Shane. 'On the coast. With his—wife, I suppose?' The word 'wife' stuck in his throat.

'Oh, yes,' said the informant, smiling. 'Folks seem to think they're a devoted couple. Deuced pretty woman, isn't she?'

He received no answer. Shane had left the bar; left it with a face whiter and grimmer than before, and a mad, crazy desire in his heart to step into his car and rush over the country to—Jalessa.

A 'devoted couple'—Eve and Gordon Veriland. But that couldn't be true.

He felt, if he did not find out—see her—make sure for himself that she still loved him in the old, blind, passionate way, he would go mad.

But he dared not go to Jalessa—in case his appearance there reacted on Evelyn and her father. Shane was frantic for the next twenty-four hours—hungry for a sight of her—afraid for her sake to go to her.

Then, that very next morning, at his hotel in

Johannesburg, there appeared a relative of Shane's —a girl cousin—Vicky Sinclair. When she met Shane in the vestibule of the hotel, he was at first amazed and then decidedly pleased to see her. Vicky was his own age, and they had seen a lot of each other in England years ago before he came out to the Colonies. She was an attractive young woman with flaming red hair, a very white skin, and brilliant greenish eyes, heavily-lidded. She was built on rather voluptuous lines; tall, stately, always well dressed; and she was amusing and clever.

Shane—unhappy—worried to death about Evelyn—greeted his cousin as a long-lost friend. He needed someone to talk to; to confide in; otherwise he was going crazy.

'I'm glad to see you, Vicky—but what are you doing in Johannesburg?' he asked, as he took her off to the veranda for a cigarette and a drink.

Vicky Sinclair eyed him appreciatively. It was two years since she had seen him, when she had last come out here on a trip with her mother. He was handsomer than ever; he looked ill, as though he had had a lot of fever, but he had always attracted her vitally, and she felt a thrill of the pulses as she realised that he was more pleased than usual to see her.

'Mother died last Christmas,' she told him. 'I'm all on my own now, Shane, and I have a bit of money, so I came out here—just to see something of you.'

'Nice of you, Vicky,' he said, without the warmth she wanted, and added, eagerly: 'I'm desperately worried at the moment, old thing. I want you to help me.'

'I'll do anything for you, Shane,' she murmured. But when the story of Evelyn tumbled out,

77

Vicky wasn't so pleased. Shane—in love—and badly in love—with a young married woman. That wasn't so good. Vicky suddenly decided that she wanted Shane for herself. They were second cousins; both free; both with money. It would be a marvellous match. She had always cared for him. Why shouldn't he care for her? It was ridiculous for him to waste his time eating out his heart for a married woman. Probably a little rotter, Vicky told herself.

Shane—needing a woman's help and sympathy—poured out the whole story. Vicky learned everything about Evelyn's father; her forced marriage; her wild, passionate affair with Shane. And the more she heard, the more convinced she became that she would hate Evelyn.

'That affair's got to blow over,' she thought. 'If only Shane got it into his head that the girl was settling down with her husband, he'd get over it and turn to me.'

She looked at his attractive, weary face with those blue, hungry eyes, and thought:

'What a lover he must be. I must make him hungry for me—*like that*!'

But aloud, her green eyes all soft with kindness and sympathy, Vicky said:

'Now look here, Shane, old thing—you mustn't worry like this. What about sending me over to Jalessa to see Mrs. Veriland?'

'Don't call her that,' he muttered.

'Evelyn, then.'

'Sending you over?' He stared at her.

'Yes. I could go as a pal and then let her know I'm your cousin and that you've sent me—I could bring you back news of her. Gordon Veriland couldn't object to that.'

Shane's tired eyes flamed. He gripped Vicky's hands.

'Vicky—what an idea! Glorious. My dear, I'm for ever in your debt if you'll help me see something of Evelyn.'

'Of course,' said Vicky sweetly. But she added to herself: 'I'll help you see nothing of her again, my dear Shane. You're going to belong to me!'

XI

Evelyn was sitting on the veranda of the hotel at Jalessa, a solitary young figure with a heart-broken look in her grey, black-lashed eyes, when the car arrived from the station bringing a new visitor to the hotel.

Vicky Sinclair had arrived.

Evelyn looked wearily at the beautiful, red-haired young woman. She did not know who she was; did not care. She cared about nothing now. Life had become a nightmare; a nightmare with Gordon as the central figure in it—constantly worrying her, hurting her, driving her mad with his possessiveness. She was at peace only when she was alone and could think of her coming baby— Shane's child—and live again in her thoughts that exquisite and thrilling dream that they had dreamed together.

She had been here in Jalessa with Gordon for nearly two months now. She was still under the impression that Shane was dead. There seemed nothing for her to live for but their child—the child which she prayed passionately would be a son, blue-eyed, black-haired, vital—like *he* had been!

Evelyn was surprised and roused from her

apathy when the red-haired stranger came up to her and said:

'Are you Mrs. Gordon Veriland?'

'I am,' said Evelyn.

'My name's Vicky Sinclair,' said the other girl, and smiled charmingly. But there was no smile in her heart. She looked down at the lovely, frail, golden-haired woman whom Shane loved and knew that it was going to be a hard task to get him away from so much allure. Yes, she knew she would hate Evelyn. But she went warily—subtlety was the order of the day. Vicky was a go-between, and if she played her cards carefully she would, inevitably, separate Shane and this woman for good and all.

She said:

'Are you alone—or is your husband here?'

'No,' said Evelyn, astonished. 'He's—away for the day. But who——'

'I'm a cousin of Shane Cargill's,' said Vicky.

The red blood swept to Evelyn's pale face and throat. She said, her heart-beats almost choking her:

'A cousin of *Shane's*?'

'Yes, he sent me along to see you.'

Evelyn stared blindly.

'*He sent you*—my God—do you mean—he's *alive*?'

'Very much so,' said Vicky. 'Hold up.'

But Evelyn lay in her chair with closed eyes and death-white cheeks. The shock of knowing that her lover still lived had been too much for her in her delicate state of health. She had fainted.

She came back to consciousness in her own bedroom, with Vicky Sinclair sitting beside her, and was like one mad with joy. She held on to the other girl's hands, sobbing wildly.

'I thought he had died—oh, I thought he had died!'

Vicky talked to her and comforted her, but she thought:

'Poor little fool. If she loves Shane as much as that, why doesn't she go to him and let her father sit in gaol?'

Vicky would have let anybody sit in gaol to suit her own ends. She was utterly selfish and unprincipled. She was already firmly determined to put an end to this affair between her cousin and Evelyn Veriland, no matter how much she made them both suffer.

Evelyn welcomed Vicky like a wanderer in the thirsty desert welcomes an oasis—a cool spring. She plied her with feverish questions about Shane— and crazy with joy that he lived—did not notice, until she grew calmer, that Vicky seemed to think Shane was not only well but quite pleased with life.

'Having quite a gay time in Johannesburg—but he sent you his love and hoped you were happy, my dear,' said Vicky sweetly.

Then some of the light faded from the grey eyes of Evelyn. She turned from Vicky and looked out at the sea. Her heart—breaking with love, with passionate hunger for Shane—ached a little; hurt a little. Shane was happy and leading a gay life. Had he forgotten all that they had meant to each other? No—she would never believe that. She turned back to Shane's cousin and talked unceasingly about him. It was good to be able to tell somebody what lay in her heart. She had been so unhappy, so repressed. Life with Gordon had been unbearable.

Vicky seemed to know everything—except about Shane's child, so Evelyn said nothing about that. But she confided most other things in the girl whom she thought was her friend.

'You see what a ghastly situation it is, Vicky. If it were not for my poor father, I could go to Shane. We were made for each other. Neither of us would mind a divorce.'

'Of course not,' murmured Vicky. 'But you couldn't let your father go to prison.'

'No,' said Evelyn desolately. 'I couldn't bear that. But one day—oh, one day, Vicky, surely I will be able to go to him. My father isn't young—if he weren't here—you understand.'

'Oh, of *course*,' said Vicky. 'If he died, you'd have no hesitation in leaving your husband for Shane.' But she thought: 'First of all, before that happens, I've got to get Shane for myself.'

'Stay with me as an old school-friend so that Gordon won't know who you are,' Evelyn begged her eagerly. Vicky assured her that she would stay. Yes, it would be easy in the course of time to make a series of remarks which would sow the seeds of suspicion in Evelyn that Shane was not so faithful as she was. And when she got back to Johannesburg, Vicky could play the same game—with Shane.

'It will be simple,' she thought that evening, after she had dressed for dinner and was going to join Evelyn in her private sitting-room. 'And Shane will turn to me—on the rebound.'

She hummed to herself as she walked along the corridor. An ebony-black servant, carrying letters on a silver salver, met her outside Evelyn's door.

'English mail, miss,' he said, grinning.

'I'll take it in to Mrs. Veriland,' said Vicky, and picked the envelopes up from the tray.

The man retreated. Vicky stopped humming and regarded, thoughtfully, the two letters with

English stamps. Now, one was for Gordon Veriland, Esq., but the other was for Mrs. Gordon Veriland, and was edged with black. A mourning letter. Mourning for whom?

A horrid little notion seized Vicky that this might be something to do with Evelyn's father. If the old man died, there would be nothing to keep Evelyn and Shane apart.

Vicky's green eyes hardened. She glanced up and down the corridor. Nobody in sight. She returned to her own bedroom, and without scruple steamed open the flap of that black-edged envelope.

It took her only a few seconds to realise that her worst fears were founded.

Charles Mayton—Evelyn's father, was dead. He had died of a stroke, and this letter was from his solicitor. He had not cabled, he said, because of the shock.

Vicky Sinclair walked up and down her room and cursed her luck. Damn, damn, *damn*! With old Mayton dead, how could she prevent Evelyn from going to Shane? Vicky was fiercely determined to make Shane her lover now.

Gradually into her cunning brain crept an insidious thought.

Supposing she gave that letter, not to Evelyn, but to *Evelyn's husband*? Supposing she made herself Gordon Veriland's ally? The last thing he desired was to lose his influence over his wife. Together they might keep that news of Mr. Mayton's death from her. Together they would keep her from Shane.

With a slow, secret smile, Vicky gummed the envelope up again and put it into her bag.

XII

Vicky did not go into Evelyn's room. She sauntered downstairs to the smoking-room which opened on to a veranda facing the starlit sea. There she found Gordon Veriland drinking a cocktail, alone. She had already been introduced to him when he returned to the hotel this evening, and he had been told that she was 'an old school-friend' of Evelyn's. He had no cause to doubt it.

He rose to his feet when Vicky approached him. He prided himself that he 'had an eye' for a pretty woman, and Evelyn's friend was damned pretty with her red hair and wonderfully white skin. He looked appreciatively at the tall, full figure in the long green chiffon dress. She wore jade ear-rings, and had a green cigarette holder between her red lips.

'Come and have a cocktail,' he said. 'What about a side-car?'

'Thanks,' murmured Vicky. 'It sounds delicious.'

She sank into a basket chair beside him. For a few moments she smoked and chatted to him. Then she threw away the cigarette-end and, putting the holder in her bag, leaned forward and addressed Gordon Veriland seriously.

'Mr. Veriland,' she said. 'I am supposed to be a pal of Evelyn's. But I want you to know that I like and respect you, and I want to be *your* friend as well.'

Gordon raised his brows. What did this mean? However, he was flattered. His rather heavy, handsome face, flushed with many drinks, creased into a smile.

'That's very charming of you—Miss Sinclair.'

'Why not "Vicky"?'

'Vicky then—and call me Gordon.'

'Thanks.' They exchanged smiles—at ease with one another.

Vicky moistened her lips with her red, pointed tongue.

'Gordon—I want you to know, also, that I—am in Evelyn's confidence.'

Veriland's gaze narrowed. He became very attentive.

'Is that so?'

'Yes. And I—happen to know everything about your marriage—its original cause—*and* Shane Cargill.'

There was no smile on Veriland's face now. It was dark red, ugly.

'What do you know about *him*?'

'Oh—lots of things. First of all that he's alive and kicking and that Evelyn still hankers after him and that any time, if she runs up against him, you may stand a good chance of losing her.'

Gordon Veriland went white with jealous rage now.

'So you think that, do you?'

'I know it.'

'And why are you telling me?'

'To warn you—and to help you keep your wife. I tell you—I like and admire you.' Lies flowed easily from Vicky's red lips. 'I want to be a good friend to you, Gordon. Evelyn's a silly little fool about Shane Cargill.'

Veriland's fingers closed so tightly round the stem of his cocktail glass that it snapped. The liquid poured on to the floor. He took no notice of it. He was breathing quickly. He had prided himself that he had mastered Evelyn, made her entirely his, wiped Shane Cargill off the slate. And now . . .

'Listen,' said Vicky in a low, rapid voice. 'I won't mince matters. You love Evelyn and want to keep her. Your one big hold on her is—her father. Isn't that so?'

'Damn it—you know a lot, don't you?'

'Enough to help *you*.'

'Well—how can you help me?'

'By giving you this,' said Vicky calmly, and handed him the black-edged letter in her bag.

Gordon Veriland took it in shaking fingers. He was shaking even more when he read it. Charles Mayton dead. *Dead*—by heaven, that meant he had no hold over his wife at all. And if, as Vicky Sinclair thought, Evelyn still loved Shane, she would go to him. He would lose all that beauty, that sweetness which he had taken by force and wanted to keep.

He heard Vicky's cool, measured voice.

'It won't do to let Evelyn know what is in that letter, will it?'

'No—by God—no.' Veriland's face was suffused.

'Then it's up to you to be clever and keep her from knowing it.'

Veriland met Vicky's gaze. He said hoarsely:

'You're no friend of Evelyn's. Why are you so anxious to help me keep her?'

'Because,' said Vicky slowly, 'I happen to be in love with Shane Cargill—and I want *him*.'

Veriland drew a deep breath.

'I see.'

'Well, are we allies?' Vicky smiled at him.

'Yes,' he said. '*Yes*.'

They were still talking, earnestly, when Evelyn came down from her room and joined them. And little did she dream that Shane's cousin, who had

86

seemed her friend, a harbinger of the most glorious and thrilling news, was a traitor in league with her husband, and that together they planned to keep from her the knowledge that her father was dead and that she was free to go to her lover.

Evelyn was almost happy that night. She went to bed early, excusing herself from Gordon and Vicky on the grounds that she had a headache. In truth, it was so that she could write to Shane. A long, long letter, throbbing with passion, with all the pent-up emotion and ecstasy and sorrow that had lain for so long locked in her heart. She would give it to Vicky to send to him.

'Shane, sweetheart, dearest of all the world,' she wrote, 'what heavenly news your cousin brought me. Shane, my darling, my darling, I thought you were dead. How perfectly wonderful to know that you're alive and that one day I may feel your arms around me and your lips on mine again. All these weeks I've suffered so—cried for you—broken myself to bits for you—ached and bled for need of you. Shane, it's been hell—wanting you back and thinking you had gone for ever. I had to give myself to *him*—for our child's sake. Oh, Shane, the torture! But I've never, in my mind, belonged to any man but you. I am still utterly yours. Shane, write to me, tell me you love me still. I couldn't bear it if you didn't. Shane, darling, only lover, can't I see you just for an hour? I want you so . . .'

Pages and pages wrote Evelyn, her heart aching and throbbing, the tears rolling down her cheeks. She sealed the letter and put it under her pillow. To-morrow she would send it to him.

She dreamed that night that he held her to his heart again; heard that husky, remembered voice, whispering 'Sweetheart' against her hair. Then the dream changed and he was standing apart from her—sneering—unlike the lover she knew and adored. When she held out a hand to him, he laughed and turned his back on her. Aghast, terrified, she awoke, and found herself in a cold sweat. She tried to console herself.

'It was only a bad dream. He loves me still—he would never turn his back on me.'

But she could not sleep peacefully again that night.

In the morning, early, she dressed and took the letter she had written—a letter that held half her heart's blood—and went along to Vicky Sinclair's room. She was anxious to talk to Vicky about *him* and get her to address this letter.

She found Vicky also up and dressed. Somewhat surprised, Evelyn glanced round the room and saw that all Vicky's luggage was packed and strapped and Vicky wore her travelling costume.

'Why—you're not going away?'

'Yes. I am catching the eleven o'clock mail train to Johannesburg.'

Vicky looked calmly and a little scornfully at Evelyn. The lovely, delicate, weary face—so marked with suffering—did not touch her. She hated Evelyn because she was the woman Shane loved. Vicky had made her plans with Gordon last night, and she was going to carry them out—ruthlessly.

Evelyn said in a breathless voice:

'Why are you going so soon? Is it to fetch Shane here to me? I've written this letter—will you give it to him?'

Vicky ignored the letter.

'No. I'm not going to fetch Shane here. Neither am I going to pass on your love-letters.'

Evelyn stood transfixed; amazed at the changed demeanour of this girl whom she had thought her friend. Vicky was entirely altered from the sympathetic confidante of yesterday.

'Vicky!' she exclaimed. 'Why, *Vicky*!'

'Let's be frank with each other,' said Vicky. 'You'd best hear the truth and know exact how the land lies. Evelyn—I'm no friend of yours—neither am I going to be a nice, useful messenger between you and my cousin. I love Shane myself. I've been in love with him for years. I came out to South Africa with the intention of marrying him.'

Evelyn went on staring, like one stupefied. The colour burnt in her cheeks and her heart beat fast and furiously. Vicky Sinclair—*in love* with Shane!

'What's more,' continued Vicky coolly, 'Shane is in love with me.'

Then the colour ebbed from Evelyn's cheeks.

'Oh, no—*no*!'

'Yes, I say. He was only infatuated with you. You led him on—a married woman—you had no right to. You're trying to ruin his life, and he feels a duty toward you. But he loves me.' Vicky's green eyes were half-closed and her lips curled viciously. 'You'd better get used to that idea and understand why he hasn't made any effort to see you all these weeks.'

Evelyn felt sick. The brutal words flung at her so pitilessly ground her down like a threshing-machine. She sank on to a chair, white and trembling, staring at Vicky with stricken eyes.

'Now,' said Vicky, 'you're going to tear up that letter—that love-letter you've written Shane, and you're going to write another—giving him up—to me!'

'No,' said Evelyn between pale, dry lips. '*No!*'

'Yes,' said Vicky relentlessly. 'You can't keep us apart. He wants to marry me and it's your duty to give him up.'

'I shall never believe he has stopped caring for me—until I hear it from his own lips,' whispered Evelyn.

'I'm damned if you're going to see him and try and wheedle him back to you—start the old infatuation,' said Vicky in a venomous tone. 'He's got to have a chance to forget you exist. Besides—you've got your husband.'

Evelyn rose to her feet, panting.

'You're a wicked creature to speak to me like this—bully me this way—when you know the whole truth.'

'Yes, I know it,' said Vicky with a hard laugh. 'And what's more, unless you write that letter and give Shane up—I'll help Gordon Veriland to ruin your father.'

Evelyn regarded her speechlessly. Such treachery, such beastliness was beyond her comprehension. Besides, she didn't believe that Shane wanted to marry this girl. Recklessly, hysterically, off her guard, Evelyn said:

'You can't separate me from Shane—you can't. I'm going to be the mother of his child—he knows it—he would never marry you under the circumstances.'

'Oh,' said Vicky slowly. 'I *see*.'

Silence. Evelyn was white, trembling, distraught. Vicky was white, too, with anger, with chagrin. She hadn't known that Evelyn was bearing Shane a child. Then she laughed. After all, that knowledge delivered Evelyn into her hands.

'Gordon Veriland doesn't know about that child, does he?'

'No. He will be told it is his.'

'If he knew,' said Vicky slowly, 'he'd be a little less keen to keep you, wouldn't he?'

Evelyn shook her golden head helplessly. She was not an adventuress; she was not used to intrigue, to lying and planning and plotting. She floundered out of her depth and the morass closed about her.

'Listen to me,' said Vicky. 'Once more, I tell you I am in love with Shane and I mean to marry him, and if you fade out of the scene he'll marry me. I'm going to fight for what I want—by foul means if I can't get it by fair. You will sit down this moment and write to Shane and tell him your affair with him is ended, finally.'

'No,' began Evelyn hoarsely.

'I say you will,' broke in Vicky. 'And in that letter you will tell him that you've become fond of your husband and anxious to live with him in peace. What's more you will tell Shane you made an error when you said you were going to have his child, and that your coming baby is *Gordon's*—do you hear?'

'No!' said Evelyn, wide-eyed, panting. 'Never! I shall never lie to Shane like that—whether he cares for me or not.'

'Right,' said Vicky. 'Then I shall go straight down to Gordon and tell him about this child. And you know what that means. Your father will go to gaol.'

Silence. Evelyn's frantic heart-beats hurt her. The waters were swirling round her, closing over her innocent head. And she saw that she was the dupe of a scheming woman; a traitor, who held her in the hollow of her hand. Perhaps it was true that Shane regretted their affair and had no further use for her. Perhaps it was true that he wanted to marry Vicky. That was bitterness enough. But to be forced to write such a letter—to lie about their child, that was too much. Yet she had sacrificed so much to save her father. Why kick at further sacrifice? And if Shane no longer loved her, what did anything matter?

She felt Vicky's firm fingers take the letter she had written to her lover.

'Well, Evelyn—shall I burn this? Will you write what I ask?'

Evelyn's fair head sank. She covered her face with her hands.

'You give me no choice,' she whispered.

Vicky's eyes glittered. She threw Evelyn's love-letter into the empty grate and put a match to it.

'You're wise, my dear,' she said. 'Much better to settle down with your husband and put Shane out of your life. You can't hope to keep him hanging on the end of a string all your life, and he'll marry me and be quite happy. You see, it's for the best.'

Evelyn lifted a face from which all hope, all youth, all beauty had been wiped.

'You've won,' she said. 'Give me a pen and a sheet of notepaper. I'll write to Shane, and then please go and I hope I never see you again.'

XIII

Vicky had wired to Shane to meet her train when she arrived from Jalessa, and it was in his car, driving to her hotel, that she carried out her plan to its cunning end and gave him Evelyn's letter.

Shane had met that train, eager and thrilled as a

boy. He was going to hear news of Evelyn, his love. He could scarcely wait to know how she was and hear that she loved him still.

But the eagerness and happiness died a chilly death at his cousin's first words. With a deep sigh and a sympathetic look in her brilliant greeny eyes, Vicky said:

'My poor Shane—not very good news, I'm afraid.'

'What!' he said hoarsely. 'Is she ill—dead?'

'Not ill,' said Vicky. 'But dead—to you.'

'Dead to *me*?'

'Yes, my dear. I'm terribly sorry this is going to be a frightful revelation—a bitter blow. But Evelyn isn't quite what you thought she was, my poor old boy.'

Shane drove a little way out of the town and pulled the big racing car up at the side of the road. His lips were set, his handsome blue eyes full of a nameless fear.

'What are you trying to tell me?' he asked his cousin roughly. 'Out with it, Vicky. What's happened? Why isn't Evelyn what I thought her?'

'Because she's forgotten you, Shane. When I got to Jalessa I wasn't welcomed. Evelyn had no wish to remember you'd ever been her lover.'

White-lipped, Shane stared at her.

'That's not true. You don't know what lovers we were. And there was our child—perhaps you don't realise——'

'I know all about that,' broke in Vicky. 'And that's one of the things you'll be most bitter about. Evelyn's a rotten little trickster. She told me, coolly, that she'd lied to you. She wasn't ever going to have your baby. If she has one, it'll be Gordon Veriland's. She crazy about him, Shane. She told me to tell you she'd changed. You've got to face it.'

He sat stunned, crushed by this news. He stared at Vicky without seeing her. It wasn't credible. Evelyn—his lily of a girl with her innocent grey eyes, her golden hair and passionate, responsive lips—a trickster—wanted—anxious to forget him—'crazy about her husband.' Evelyn fickle, inconstant, denying that he was the father of her child.

'I don't believe it!' he broke out violently. 'I'll go to Jalessa to-night—to-morrow—find out for myself.'

'Read what she says, Shane. Surely you've got more pride——'

The cool, insidious voice of Vicky trickled into his fevered mind. He opened, with shaking fingers, the letter which Evelyn had sent him. When he saw that familiar writing and saw what she had to say—indisputable proof of her faithlessness—he nearly went mad.

'Please forget I ever existed and don't try to see me or communicate with me again. I want to settle down with my husband. I am absolutely happy with him now and I know now that it is *Gordon* who is the father of my coming child. Good-bye, EVELYN.'

Proof enough. All that Vicky said was right. That fellow who had heard that the 'Verilands were a devoted couple' had been right.

Evelyn wanted to be forgotten—did she? All right—he wasn't going to crawl to her and waste himself on her. He'd wasted too much agony and heart-break over her as it was. *His* Evelyn—*his* son.

What a farce! Shane laughed. He tore Evelyn's note in pieces.

'To hell with it,' he said. 'That ends it, Vicky—if *that's* what she's like.'

'I'm afraid it is.'

'And I believed in her—adored her!'

'You'll get over it, Shane. Don't let her have the laugh of you. Show her how little you mind.'

'I wish I could!' He shook from head to foot. He was raw with disappointment, with misery.

Then Vicky played her last card.

She put an arm about his shoulders. She leaned her red head against him and said in a throbbing voice:

'Shane, Shane, I'm so terribly in love with you—always have been—I'm not ashamed to say so. I can't bear you to be hurt like this—can't bear the idea that that rotten little beast, Evelyn, has let you down. Shane—can't I comfort you? Won't you let me try?'

He looked down at her white, upturned face. It looked soft, attractive. The green eyes were hot with passion for him. Vicky loved him, did she? He needed a woman's love. He'd lost Evelyn—for ever. And all these months he'd been hungry, lonely, fretting for her.

Why not show Evelyn—Mrs. Gordon Veriland, *damn her*—that she couldn't take him in those white hands of hers and break him in pieces just for a whim?

He caught Vicky blindly in his arms.

'Do you really love me, Vicky?'

'Terribly,' she said, panting. 'I've always wanted you—always, Shane.'

'Will you marry me?'

Her heart jumped.

'Do you want me to?'

'Yes, and to hell with everything.'

So she'd got him—on the rebound—just as she'd planned. Got him when he was raw with disappointment and hurt vanity. She wanted to laugh with triumph. But she gave a little sob of passion and pulled that dark, attractive head of his down to her flaming one.

'I love you madly. I'll make up to you for all that you've suffered.'

He set his lips to hers in a passionate kiss. But if his body thrilled to hers, his mind was dead—his heart ice-cold. There was nothing but bitterness in his soul. He had loved Evelyn and he knew that till he died he would not be able to forget her. And because he loved her so much he hated her for what he thought she had done to him.

Two days later the South African papers published the announcement of an interesting engagement between Shane Cargill, of Johannesburg, and Victoria Sinclair, of London. The wedding was to take place in a month's time.

Shane—having burnt his boats—plunged into reckless gaiety. He accompanied his beautiful, red-haired fiancée from one party to another in Johannesburg—feverishly trying to put the memory of Evelyn from him.

And meanwhile, in Jalessa, Evelyn lay at death's door.

For a week or two after Vicky Sinclair had left Jalessa, Evelyn had returned to that state of hopeless despair which she had known when she had thought Shane was dead. But then she had felt justified in grieving, in breaking her heart for him. Her memories of him had been all lovely and ecstatic ones. Now there was so much bitterness.

Shane no longer belonged to her. He was alive—but as good as dead to her—worse. And day and night she worried over the letter she had sent him. She told herself repeatedly that she had done it for Daddy's sake—poor old Daddy who might so easily be sent to prison. But she could not bear the thought of the lies she had told Shane about her change of feeling for him, and their child.

Gordon watched her closely. He saw that she was in a nervy, hysterical condition and he was anxious about her health. He left her alone, those days—fearing to drive her to the pitch of suicide. But he carried out his part of Vicky's plans carefully. And when she commented on the fact that she had not heard from her father lately, he told her not to worry—that the mails were delayed this time of the year.

Then, one black, unforgettable day for Evelyn, she opened a Johannesburg newspaper and saw the announcement of Shane Cargill's forthcoming wedding to Vicky Sinclair.

Her heart seemed to break in two when she read it. At least Vicky had spoken the truth about that. Shane had forgotten her. He loved Vicky and he was going to marry her.

Evelyn, after days and nights of brooding, of suffering, went a little crazy that day. Shane, her lover, father of her child, was going to marry Vicky. She could not tolerate the idea. She rushed, like one demented from the hotel, down to the seashore and walked blindly for miles along the side of the blue, shining sea. She walked until she was exhausted, then, in a little white sandy cove, flung herself down on the warm sand and burst into tears.

'Shane, Shane, *Shane!*'

She sobbed his name in an agony of wounded love and despair. She lay, exhausted, half-conscious, not caring whether she lived or died.

Gordon Veriland found her, an hour later, after an anxious search—still lying there on the beach, with the warm waves lapping round her. But she was insensible and did not know that she was in danger of being drowned.

Veriland, for the first time in his selfish life, was genuinely concerned. He carried her back to the hotel—sent for a doctor. And for many bitter days and nights after that Evelyn lay seriously ill in her hotel bedroom, too ill to move or speak, or to worry now about Shane or anybody.

She looked frail because of her blonde colouring and slenderness, but she was constitutionally strong and somehow or other managed to pull through those critical days. She struggled back to health, indifferent to everything and everybody, with great grey eyes too big for her white, delicate face, and bitterness smouldering behind her apparent resignation to her fate.

When the doctors told her that she was not now to be a mother, she was beyond caring. She had wanted Shane's son once, passionately, fervently. But now, as Shane was to become Vicky's husband, she did not want it. She was glad that she was not going to have a child.

When Gordon suggested that they should leave Jalessa and go back to the gaiety of town-life, she did not protest.

'If you wish it,' she said.

Her utter indifference to everything made the man a little uneasy and ashamed of himself. But his desire to possess, to keep that frail, haunting beauty, killed the decent feelings in him.

98

'A little amusement will buck you up, my dear child,' he said. 'We'll go to Johannesburg and then over to Algiers and Egypt for the winter, shall we?'

'If you like,' she said in the same dull voice.

And she wondered, as she felt so dead, how long it would be before the memory of Shane died. For even now she could not forget a single kiss that he had given her; nor a single hour that they had spent in each other's arms.

She was fretting now about lack of news from her father.

'Can Daddy be ill or something?' she said to Gordon as they travelled to Johannesburg, as soon as she was fit for the long journey.

'No, no,' said Veriland. 'As a matter of fact, I had a letter from him while you were ill, darling. He's doing a cruise in the Mediterranean, and said he won't write much till he gets back to London.'

Evelyn accepted this story. Why not? It never entered her head to suspect that Gordon was deliberately keeping the news of her father's death from her.

So they returned to 'life' at Johannesburg. And from the hour they entered the city, memories of Shane and of their first meeting here tormented Evelyn—cut like a hot knife through the cold wall of indifference which she had built about herself.

To please Gordon, she accompanied him to a ball the very night after their arrival. A brilliant, glittering affair, given by the South African millionaire diamond magnate, and attended by the richest business men and prettiest women in Johannesburg.

One of the loveliest figures was Mrs. Gordon Veriland. She was exquisite in a white satin 'Victorian dress,' with a jewelled belt at the small

99

waist, and long full skirt richly sewn with seed pearls. There were priceless creamy pearls about her throat; diamonds clasping her arms; white orchids on her shoulder; and she wore a tight little white velvet coat. All white—curiously virginal— and cold as the snows. Every man in the room looked at her; drank in the sight of so much loveliness. But she was a passionless lily. And none could have dreamed that once she had trembled for love and ecstasy— sobbed with the passionate emotion of loving—in Shane Cargill's arms!

She danced the first few dances with her husband. He—inflamed with her beauty and proudly possessive—whispered against her ear:

'You lovely thing—are you going to be kind to me to-night? I haven't asked for a single kiss—for weeks.'

Evelyn shuddered, and her face was as pale as her dress; but she said, wearily:

'Anything you wish.'

But she thought:

'What does my body matter? He can never have my heart. I wonder if Shane is married yet?'

Then the blood scorched her face and throat fiercely. The lily became a flaming rose. Over Gordon's shoulder she saw a tall, sun-browned, blue-eyed man enter the room with a red-haired girl in a black lace dress.

Shane. Shane and Vicky Sinclair. Or—was she Vicky Cargill by now?

Evelyn soon knew. A woman dancing close to her said:

'Here comes Shane Cargill—the most attractive man in Johannesburg. That's his fiancée, and they're being married to-morrow.'

Evelyn's heart hurt badly. So—Shane was to be

married to Vicky to-morrow. This was his wedding-eve.

She could not dance any more. She made an excuse to her husband and left him, and walked blindly out of the room. She had to pass Shane Cargill to get out of the ball-room. He saw her and stiffened in every limb. God, what a host of bitter, passionate memories surged back when he saw that exquisite figure in white, that golden head, that haunting face.

He, himself, was thin, burnt up with too much gaiety, reckless drinking. He had been trying to forget Evelyn and devote himself to Vicky, who was to become his wife.

He saw Evelyn again and knew indisputably that he could not marry Vicky while Evelyn lived, and coupled with that feeling came intense anger against Evelyn—resentment against her for the thing she had done to him.

She met his gaze, and for one feverish instant they stared at each other. He made a gesture toward her, but she cut him dead, and with her golden head held high walked out of the room.

Vicky pulled at Shane's arm. She was furious that Evelyn should be here—she knew perfectly well what effect the sight of her had upon Shane.

'Come on—let's dance, old thing,' she said.

'If you'll pardon me one moment,' said Shane, and with tight lips and grim blue eyes he swung on his heel and left the ball-room.

He was going to follow Evelyn, find her; speak to her; make her pay for cutting him, make her pay for everything that she'd done to him, whatever the issue. No woman on earth was going to treat Shane Cargill like that and not pay for it.

'Shane!' began Vicky furiously.

Then a tall young man barred her from following Shane.

'*Hello, Vicky*—fancy meeting *you!*'

An old pal. Vicky was forced to stay and greet him; talk to him. But she looked with angry eyes over his shoulder and watched Shane vanish into the hall. She knew that he was following Evelyn.

Evelyn had fetched her little Victorian coat from the ladies' room and rushed into the moonlit garden of the hotel where the big ball was in progress. She was distracted; pale as her gown—all the paler for the searching moonlight that played upon her lovely face. Her heart was hammering; her hands dry and shaking.

Heavens, what a wild flood of regrets, of misery, of despair the sight of Shane Cargill had unlocked in her. She was drowning in it; scarcely capable of clear thought or calm action. She only knew she could not stay in that ball-room with her husband and see Shane dancing with Vicky, to whom he was to be married—to-morrow.

She hurried away from the hotel down a terrace and into a secluded part of the garden, where giant palms cast fantastic shadows on the moon-silvered lawns and there were flowers in wild profusion and loveliness.

She must be alone. And thinking herself alone, she paused and covered her face with her slender, trembling hands.

'Oh, oh—oh!' she moaned. 'I still love him. I am so absolutely *his*. Oh, I thought I had got over it—that I wouldn't suffer any more. But now that I see him I'm in torment and I can't *bear* it!'

Then she heard a well-remembered voice.

'Eve!'

She let her hands fall. Pale as death, shaking

from her golden head to her small white-slippered feet she looked up—into the hard blue eyes of Shane.

'You!' she whispered.

'Yes, I followed you.'

'Why?'

'Why did you cut me? How dared you walk by me—like that—with your head in the air—as though you loathed me—as though we were strangers—as though you had never lain in my arms?'

His voice was savage, naked with pain, raw with resentment. She cried out:

'Oh, stop—please!'

'Do you think that I'll let you get away with that? Do you think I'm going to be cut dead—for you and Gordon Veriland to sneer at—after the way you treated me? Oh, my God, I would have thought you were more faithful to me!'

She stared, her sweet mouth round and open with astonishment. Then the red blood stung her cheeks and her eyes blazed with an anger that matched his.

'How dare you? How dare you speak to me like this—when you are marrying Vicky Sinclair—to-morrow?'

'I'm not so sure that I am.'

'I happen to know you are.'

He said through clenched teeth:

'But it happens that I still want *you*, Eve. You're rotten to the core—unfaithful to every vow you made me. You've cheated me—even of my son—but I still want your lovely, treacherous body, and I'm going to take you whether you want me or not.'

She put a hand to her lips.

'You're mad.'

'Perhaps—but not so crazy that I'm going to sit

103

down and allow you and Veriland to crow over me—damn you both.'

'*Shane!*' she panted.

He laughed and caught her close. For a moment she felt the burning touch of his lips upon her mouth. A hard, furious caress from lips which she had thought would never touch hers again. Then his arms picked her up wholly—carried her speechless, dumbfounded, through that moonlit deserted garden to the drive, where a row of cars had been parked by the visitors. Evelyn cried out, once:

'How dare you? What are you doing? You're right off your head.'

But he did not answer, and kept her tightly in his arms—so tightly that she could scarcely breathe. Some of the seed pearls from her gorgeous, glittering dress, broke and scattered on to the grass. They reached the big white racing car which was familiar enough to Evelyn—hadn't he come to her villa in the mountains in that car, day after day, in the past? It awoke a host of painful, throbbing memories in her. But what was Shane doing this for? He was mad—reckless—and it was all quite incomprehensible to her.

He put her into the car, climbed into the driver's seat and slammed the door. Then he switched on and set the powerful engine humming. A moment later they were away—at breakneck speed —rushing along the moon-whitened road, leaving a cloud of dust and exhaust behind them.

In the car, Evelyn crouched, panting, wide-eyed.

'You must be crazy! Hadn't you better stop?'

'So that you can go back to Veriland and laugh? No, my dear. Once you belonged to me and you're going to belong to me again. To hell with all of you—Vicky included.'

'That's nice—for your fiancée!' Evelyn gave a hysterical laugh.

Shane did not answer that. He stared ahead of him with those very blue eyes, like stones, she thought, in his lean brown face. Studying him now at leisure she noted how thin he had grown—how much older. Had these last few months told on him? But why? He did not care for her. He had forgotten her—for another woman. She was full of aching tenderness for him, but she was angry, too, and anger conquered for the moment. The impudence of it—the sheer insolence—to carry her off by force under Gordon's very nose.

Where were they going? How would it end? Her eyes, black with feverish excitement, suddenly turned to him.

'Shane—stop—take me back. You've no right——'

'Be quiet,' he broke in harshly.

'I shall jump out,' she began hysterically.

'No you won't.'

He kept his right hand on the steering wheel and put the other arm about her. It was like steel—holding her down. She was furious; yet the old wild thrill surged through her slender body. The strength, the devilment of this man! She had adored him for it in the past. She adored him to-night. The old wild fever for him was still burning furiously, whatever he did or had done. She ceased to fight or to try to understand why he was behaving in this fashion. She sat quiescent, eyes closed, the warm wind rushing against her face as the big car raced through the night.

Shane drove on. He was in one of his worst moods; reckless and regardless of the havoc his departure with Evelyn would raise; of the chaos left behind them. He only knew that this slender, grey-eyed, golden-haired woman was his; that he still wanted her to madness, and that he was not going to give her up for any reason on earth.

For an hour, without speaking another word, keeping his one arm about her, he drove—out of Johannesburg and up the mountains. There he owned a shooting-box, a small, rather attractive bungalow built of pine-logs, and fitted out for two or more men who were out for a few days' shooting. It was fitted with every convenience that money could buy, and there was always tinned food in the larder for an emergency and camp beds made up ready to sleep in. To this place Shane drove Evelyn. It looked lonely and deserted—in the most remote part of the mountains, surrounded by trees. Everything looked wild and desolate in the bright moonlight.

It was a coolish night. It never grew warm until sunrise up here in the mountains, and when Evelyn climbed from the car she was stiff and shivering in her white Victorian dress and velvet coat.

Shane unlocked the front door.

'Go in,' he said.

'Hadn't you better put an end to this joke and take me back?' she began.

He caught hold of her, laughed, and carried her in, his lips stifling the protest from hers.

'I'm glad you think it's a joke, my dear. But you'll soon discover that it isn't,' he said.

Evelyn's heart pounded, and she felt faint when he set her on her feet again. She stood dumb, holding a finger to the lips which he had hurt with that last, fierce kiss. He was going too far. She wouldn't stand it.

He lit an oil-lamp and put it on the table. Startled, she looked round and saw in the dim golden-light a delightful room—polished pine floor, walls hung with animals' skins, rifles, ivories, hunting trophies. There was a big open fireplace, a bookcase full of novels, Persian rugs, striped silk curtains, and through an open door a bedroom, simply but attractively furnished.

'What is this place?' she asked.

'My shooting-box,' said Shane. '"Mountain Lodge" is the name. Your home for the present. It's a bit chilly. But there are plenty of dry logs in the outhouse. I'll get some and we'll light a fire. Then we'll raid the larder and have some supper. I'm hungry. When we're warm and fed—we can sit in front of the fire in each other's arms like we used to do——'

There was no tenderness in his voice, only irony and bitterness in his eyes.

Evelyn looked up at him with a bewildered face.

'Shane—what are you doing this for? Why have you brought me here?'

'To make you pay, my dear.'

'Pay—for what?'

'For the way you treated me and cheated me.'

Silence a moment. Her heart-beats hurt her. She kept her dark grey eyes riveted on his hard, bitter face. Then she said:

'You aren't sane. In what way did I cheat you?'

'You promised to love me always—belong to me always. You told me you were to be the mother of my child. Then you wrote me that cruel letter—chucking me on one side—informing me that you'd grown attached to your husband—that the child was his. Oh, my *God*!'

'And what about you—your engagement to that

107

girl? Weren't you easily consoled? You sent her to me with brutal messages—broke my heart in two by telling her to ask me to step aside and allow you to marry her.'

'That's a lie!' he broke out hotly.

'What's more,' continued Evelyn, 'she used the information you had given her about my father to bully me—to force my hand. She swore to tell Gordon about our child that would have meant he'd put Daddy in prison unless I gave you up and denied that the child was yours.'

It was Shane's turn to stare. He went livid.

'Evelyn—is that true? Did Vicky do *that*?'

'Yes.' She sank into a chair and burst into tears, overwrought, still far from strong after her recent illness. 'I loved you, Shane—never stopped loving you; and when I thought you no longer wanted me—that you wanted Vicky—I did what I was asked. I gave you up.'

Shane stood staring at her, speechless with astonishment and wrath as gradually the real facts were unfolded to him. He questioned Evelyn rapidly. And with every answer the truth grew more lucid. He understood. Vicky had lied. Vicky was a vile traitor. She had been double-faced—incredibly base, and had lied to and tricked both of them. And that was the girl he had meant to marry in order to show Evelyn that he did not care.

He looked down at Evelyn's bent gold head. He saw her beautiful face bathed in tears, her delicate body shaken with wild weeping.

'I still love you—always will. I nearly killed myself. Our baby didn't live—oh, Shane, Shane!'

Then he went down on his knees beside her, wrapped both arms about her, and buried his dark head against her lap.

'Sweetheart—oh, Sweetheart—what a frightful mistake I've made! And I love you better than life itself, and always will.'

'You do still care? You don't love—Vicky?'

'I loathe her. I could kill her for what she has done to both of us. I sent her to you with messages of love and hope and she betrayed me. Eve, my darling, Loveliest! Forgive me—if you can!'

'Forgive me, if I hurt you with that cruel letter. Every word I wrote stabbed my heart like a knife,' she said, her tears falling thickly, her hands threading through his hair. 'We were both misled, Shane, darling. But now we know that we love each other still.'

'Much more!' he said.

'Much more!' she whispered. 'Oh, Shane!'

He stood up and pulled her into his embrace. He kissed her lips, her cheeks, her hair, her throat—kissed her tears away—covered her with frantic, passionate caresses.

'How thin you are—how ill you must have been. Oh, Evelyn—my Sweet—my Sweet!'

'I nearly died, but in your arms I am well again, dearest.'

Cheek to cheek, breathless, ecstatic, they clung to each other. Then Evelyn said in a quivering voice:

'We've burnt our boats—coming here together—they may trace us in time—and there's Daddy. Shane, haven't we been a little mad?'

'It's a glorious madness, Sweetheart, and I can't take you back now,' he said huskily.

'Do you mean we are to—stay here?'

'Yes. How can we go back now?'

He glanced at his watch. He laughed grimly.

'A new day, Evelyn. It was meant to be my wedding-day. My wedding—with that foul, treacherous woman—my own cousin, I'm ashamed to say.'

'You won't marry her now?'

'Knowing that you still love me and after what she did to you—to me? My God, no!' He laughed again, and held her closer. He was flushed under his tan; bright-eyed, all the old fever and passion for Evelyn throbbing anew in his veins.

Evelyn lay against his heart, her face rapt and passionate. This knowledge that Shane was still utterly her lover was ecstasy indeed. After all the heartbreak, the suffering, the needing him, it was heaven. And heaven to be here, along with him, instead of a slave to Gordon and his whims. She paled at the thought of Gordon.

'Shane, I'm frightened.'

'Of what, Sweetheart?'

'Of—my husband.'

'He won't find us.'

'But this way may react on Daddy.'

'No—Veriland won't do anything until he finds you again—he won't want to lose his hold over you.'

'That's true. Then dare I stay with you here—and wait?'

'Yes, my Sweet—I can't let you go.'

'But, Shane——' Her voice shook. 'We must be—good—until we know what is happening. I'm so much more Gordon's wife than I used to be. You understand.'

Shane flushed darkly.

'I don't want to think of it—remember it. But I'll do anything on earth you ask me. I won't touch a hair of your beautiful head if you don't want me to.'

'You know how much I want you to.' She stroked his cheek, wistfully, with her delicate fingers. 'But until we know where we are and what's going to happen——'

'Yes, all right, darling—I understand.'

'I adore you,' she said passionately.

'I shall never rest until you belong to me,' he said, and set his lips to her upturned, lovely mouth.

During that kiss Evelyn knew a contentment she had not felt for long, bitter months. But through it all crept the uneasy remembrance of her idolised father—his safety, which she believed lay in her hands. *And she was afraid.*

XIV

It only took Vicky Sinclair half an hour in which to discover that Shane had gone, and she took it for granted that Evelyn had gone with him. She searched the hotel and gardens, madly, furiously, her face livid, her lips bitten through, and with a murderous feeling in her heart for Evelyn.

She found out that Shane's car had vanished from the parking-place. She then went straight to Gordon Veriland. He, on his part, had been distractedly searching the place for his wife.

Vicky and Gordon met, face to face, on the moonlit terrace outside the hotel, about an hour after Shane and Evelyn had disappeared. Veriland by this time was badly frightened. Evelyn had vanished as though the earth had swallowed her up, and he was never quite sure of what she would do to herself—of how far his possessive cruelty would drive her.

He was glad to see Vicky.

'Do you happen to know where my wife is?'

Vicky—a handkerchief to her lips—laughed hoarsely.

'Do you happen to know where my future husband is?'

'Cargill, you mean?'

'Yes, Shane. He's vanished.'

'So has my wife.'

Vicky laughed again—venomously.

'It's pretty obvious, isn't it? They've gone together.'

Veriland's face became suffused; he breathed noisily.

'By heaven—if I thought that——'

'You can take it for granted. I saw him follow her out of the hotel.'

'Then they *have* gone together.'

'It looks like it.'

'For a ride only.' Veriland licked his lips. 'It must be just for a ride. They'll come back.'

'They'd better,' said Vicky, swallowing hard. 'Oh, they'd better. I'm to be married to Shane tomorrow. Gordon Veriland, if you want your wife as much as I want Shane——'

'You can take it for granted that I do.' He almost snarled the words.

'Then we'll wait and see—*if* they come back.'

'Can she have heard——?'

'That her father is dead? No—how can she?'

'That's right,' muttered Veriland. 'She can't know. I've still got that as a lever.'

They waited, pacing that terrace for an hour, two hours, three hours. They were both enraged, helpless. Not a soul had seen Shane drive away or could give them a single clue.

The night passed and the dawn came. And Gordon Veriland in his hotel, and Vicky in hers, knew that those two did not mean to come back. They faced the fact, raging impotently.

They met again the following day.

'It's now certain that Evelyn and Shane have gone off together,' said Vicky. She was a haggard wreck after a sleepless night. 'To-day is my wedding-day. And Shane's quit me. Gordon Veriland, if you don't help me to trace those two——'

'I'll help you,' broke in the man harshly. 'What do you think? Don't I want my wife back? I'm never going to give her up to Cargill—never, *never*!'

'Good,' said Vicky between her teeth. 'Then we'll work on this together. You'll give me your promise that when we find them—you won't let Shane have her—you won't divorce her?'

'Never,' repeated Veriland. 'When I do find her she'll pay for this—and she'll never get a divorce. I swear it.'

In a measure Vicky was comforted by that. But it could not give her the bridegroom who had shirked his marriage with her this day.

Raw with humiliation, she made public the news that 'the wedding was postponed owing to the sudden illness of Shane Cargill.'

And nobody knew the truth.

Meanwhile Gordon Veriland and Vicky worked feverishly to trace the pair who had vanished so mysteriously, so completely, in the night.

Vicky knew nothing about Shane's shooting-box in the mountains. She went to all his other properties inside Johannesburg and out of it. But Shane was to be found nowhere.

Five days passed.

Then, suddenly, on the sixth day, news came with dramatic suddenness.

Vicky, who had almost given up hope, was chatting in the lounge of her hotel with a new arrival—

a woman who had just come with her husband. They had motored, she told Vicky, from the mountains.

'We ran out of water and stopped to fill up the car at the cutest little shooting-box you ever saw in South Africa,' said this woman, who was of the garrulous type. 'And, my dear, the lodge was occupied by the most *interesting* couple—such a handsome pair—terribly in love with each other.'

'Oh, indeed,' said Vicky indifferently.

But the indifference changed to absorbing interest when her informant added:

'Honeymooners, I guess. We don't know the name, but he called her "Eve" and she called him "Shane"—and I thought him so good-looking, but my husband couldn't take his eyes off her.'

Vicky, white to the lips with excitement, and gripping the sides of her chair, said:

'Can you tell me where this shooting-box is?'

'Why, surely.'

Then Vicky knew that the search for Shane and Evelyn was at an end. Ten minutes later she left the hotel and went to Gordon Veriland.

'Now,' she said. '*Now we've got them.* And you're going to that lodge in the mountains at once, to get *your wife* away from *my man.*'

XV

Gordon Veriland's arrival at Mountain Lodge, so unexpectedly, six days after the 'elopement' put an end to the most wonderful, peaceful, happy week of Evelyn's life.

She had been perfectly contented—just dreaming away the golden hours in that lovely, solitary mountain place with her lover.

114

The happiness had been shadowed, perhaps, by the knowledge that she did not and could not yet belong to him entirely—and always there was the niggling fear in her heart for her father's safety. Again and again she said to Shane:

'I can't let Daddy down.'

And every time Shane held her close and said:

'My Sweet, I will never ask you to do that. And we couldn't either of us be happy knowing the poor old man was in gaol.'

When they saw Gordon's fast car arriving in a cloud of dust, the lovers, both white and grim about the eyes and lips, prepared for a storm.

'So he's found us,' said Shane between his teeth. 'And now for the peroration.'

'Oh, Shane, Shane—our peace is over,' she said, and clung to him, cold and shivering.

'My Sweet, how the devil am I to deal with him, knowing what I do about your father?'

'That's the trouble and tragedy,' she said, and she felt sick and terrified when she saw her husband's big figure, so painfully familiar, emerge from the car and come toward them.

They waited hand in hand in front of the little lodge which had been a paradise for them for six glorious days.

Gordon Veriland came up to them. His gaze swept past his old enemy to his wife. He saw her flinch and whiten, and gloried in it. He still had her in his power. Thank heaven she did not know about her father's death.

'Well, Evelyn,' he said. 'I've found you.'

'Gordon—listen,' she said, and spoke bravely, although her heart failed her when she read the venom, the utter lack of mercy, in his eyes. 'I admit

I've done wrong in running away with Shane, but——'

'I carried her off by force,' interrupted Shane grimly. 'And I'll do it again—*damn you, Veriland.*'

'Look here!' began Gordon furiously.

'Wait,' said Evelyn, and stepped in between them. 'Gordon, listen—I appeal to you. Shane and I love each other and——'

'You happen to be my wife,' broke in Veriland. 'And Cargill belongs to Miss Sinclair. Now, Evelyn, let's have no more of this nonsense. You're coming along back with me, and you're not going to see Cargill again as long as you live.'

He took her arm. She wrenched it away.

'I won't go with you.'

'No,' said Shane, putting an arm about her. 'Veriland, it's time *you* put an end to this filthy business. She isn't going with you. She's going to stay with me and you've got to give her a divorce.'

'Oh, have I?' Veriland laughed harshly.

'Yes, Gordon—please—have a little mercy,' added Evelyn. 'Let me go.'

'Never while I live.'

'Then I'll keep her,' said Shane, raging, aching to get at the other man with his fists.

'I think not.'

Veriland whipped a sheet of paper from his coat-pocket. It was a cablegram—carefully written on. He handed it to Evelyn.

'See that? That's all ready to send to my solicitors in London.'

Evelyn's large grey eyes saw and took in every word that was written in her husband's small, cramped hand on that cablegram. It was a detailed authorisation for them to take proceedings against Charles Mayton, her father, for obtaining money from Gordon Veriland on forged securities.

In other words, that cable, when it reached London, thought Evelyn, would send her father straight to prison. The father who had relied upon her to save him.

'Well,' said Veriland harshly. 'Are you coming back with me, Evelyn, or does that cable go off—to-day?'

XVI

Shane's temper—which he had been trying to hold in control—burst forth. He sprang between Evelyn and Veriland and tore the cablegram from the latter's hand and crumpled it into a ball, which he flung savagely on the ground.

'Damn you for a filthy swine—a rotten coward, Veriland!' he panted. 'To bully a woman—force her—in such a fashion. My God, I——'

'Now, Cargill,' broke in Gordon, stepping back a trifle nervously. 'Steady on. It's no use calling me names, and it won't alter my point of view. I want my wife just as much as you want her.' He laughed coarsely. 'And, damn it, she *is* my wife and not yours. As for tearing the cablegram—don't worry. I can write a dozen more and I shall send the facsimile of this one, within an hour, unless my wife comes back to me.'

'You——' Shane's hoarse, furious voice choked on the name which he called the other man. He felt Evelyn's soft little hand against his lips; seized it and kissed it fiercely, despite the fact that Veriland glared at him. 'Oh, my darling!' he added under his breath. 'My darling!'

'Don't lose control, Shane,' she said huskily. 'If you do it will only make things worse for me, and

117

he's right. Nothing will alter his point of view—
he's just crazy on this business of keeping me. He's
got the whip hand on us. Shane, darling—because
of Daddy, and it will only reflect on poor Daddy
and me if you lose your temper with Gordon.'

'The wisest speech you've been known to make,
my dear,' said Veriland, with a sneer.

Shane bit his lower lip until it bled. He was pale
as death under his bronze; shaking with fury. He
wanted to get his fingers round Veriland's throat
and choke him. The damnable cowardice of the
whole affair!

'Look here, Veriland,' he said, swallowing pride
and rage for Evelyn's sake. 'Play straight over this
thing, for God's sake. Whatever you do, be decent
about it. It isn't straight—this forcing Evelyn's
hand through her father—it's damned crooked.'

Veriland averted his gaze and had the grace to
flush. But his own temper flared up. He was not
going to be taught his business by Evelyn's lover.

'You go to hell,' he said. 'It isn't your affair. It's
my wife's and mine.'

Shane made a gesture of hopelessness with his
hand. Evelyn, very white and straight, looked from
him to her husband. *Her husband!* The bitterness
of that knowledge. There he was—a blustering,
pompous, selfish creature—greedy and mean and
even unprincipled—stooping to any cowardly
action in order to keep her youth and beauty for
himself. How could she tolerate living with him—
going back to him—after these few heavenly days
of sweet companionship with Shane in this sunlit
mountain retreat?

A mist of anguish blotted both men from her
vision. She covered her face with her hands. Shane
gave her a troubled, passionate look, and then

touched her fair, silky head with his hand.

'My dear, why should you go back to him and sacrifice yourself continually for your father?'

She looked up at him—eyes full of tears.

'I must, Shane. I can't let Daddy go to prison.'

'You're sending yourself to prison and me to hell instead, beloved.'

'Oh, I know,' she whispered, trembling. 'Don't enlarge on it—it's unbearable enough. But I can't let an old man like Daddy suffer. Seven years in gaol. Shane, he's sensitive and delicate. He'd never stand it. If he died in prison I'd feel I'd murdered him. I can't risk that. Better for me to give up my lover and stay with Gordon—than feel myself a murderess. Neither you nor I would be happy ever again—would we?'

'I suppose not,' he said, but his heart—loving her fiercely—rebelled against the injustice of the position.

Gordon Veriland moved a step away from them and busied himself lighting a cigarette. He was doing an incredibly base thing—parting these two who loved each other so passionately, and cheating Evelyn of the truth. He knew perfectly well that Charles Mayton was dead and buried and beyond suffering—out of reach of revenge. But any decent instincts that stirred in Veriland when he witnessed Evelyn's heroic surrender of her own happiness for her father's sake were blunted by his desire for her.

He would not give her up to Cargill. He had always loathed Shane. They were old enemies. No, he was damned if he would let Evelyn slip through his hands now.

'Let's put an end to this scene, Evelyn,' he said gruffly. 'You know where you stand. Come back with me and promise not to see Cargill again and that cable won't ever be sent to my solicitors.'

Evelyn drew a shuddering breath. She nerved herself for the ordeal in front of her.

'Yes, very well,' she whispered. 'I'll—come.'

She turned and walked into the lodge, stumbling a little because her tears blinded her. Shane followed, his heart raw and hot with resentment. He was not only agonised by the thought of losing her, but distracted at the idea that she was going to suffer. He knew her gentle, sensitive nature; knew that every fibre of her being would be jarred and hurt, forced back into her husband's arms. It was an intolerable thought to her lover.

'Eve,' he cried, 'Sweetheart—*Sweetheart!*'

She turned and rushed into his arms. She clung to him frantically, sobbing as though her heart would break.

'Shane, oh, darling, darling, isn't it too cruel? Shane, I love you so. I can't bear to leave you. I've been so happy here with you, and you've been wonderful to me.'

He crushed her close, groaning, covered her face, her throat, her golden hair with passionate kisses, showered a hundred caresses upon her.

'My Sweet—my Loveliest. I've been so happy too. It's a ghastly business—worse than cruel. It's so horrible for you to have to live with that swine. My darling, how can I endure the thought? I'd like to kill him!'

'Hush—Shane darling, don't. It's no use. Don't think too much about it. I must go—and there's an end to it.'

'But you're mine,' he said hoarsely. He held her at arm's length and looked at her with bloodshot eyes. 'You're mine—every sweet particle of you—

and you always will be. You always will love me. Swear it, Eve.'

'I swear it,' she said. 'Whatever happens—I'll always love you, Shane. I may have to live with Gordon, but he'll never have my mind, my soul, my heart. They belong to you—absolutely!'

He caught her close again. Their hearts beat together in the same tune. Their lips met and clung in desperate kisses.

She put up her hands and caressed his dark head; looked at him, as though she would imprint the memory of every feature upon her mind and keep it—a living picture—to comfort her.

'My darling, darling Shane! No lovers have ever loved each other so much,' she whispered brokenly.

'No woman was ever so sweet as you,' he said. 'So dear, so brave. Oh, my dear, what a lucky man your father is—to have such a daughter to sacrifice so much for his sake.'

She buried her face in the curve of his arm and wept passionately.

'It's really good-bye this time, darling.'

'I know,' he said hoarsely. 'It's like death to me.'

'And to me, Shane dearest.'

A cold, bitter, venomous voice broke in upon this scene and made the tragic and despairing lovers draw apart.

'All very charming—but what about me?'

Vicky Sinclair stood in the doorway, Gordon just behind her. She had followed in her own car, afraid that Veriland might not succeed in separating the lovers without her assistance. Shane and Evelyn, with clasped hands, stood side by side and faced her. She was cool and debonair—perfectly turned out in a well-cut shantung suit with a big white hat on her auburn head. She looked handsome enough to please any man, but to Shane she had become as repellent as a snake. She had betrayed his trust and helped to make Evelyn suffer cruelly, and it was more than he could ever forgive or forget.

'*You've* done enough harm, haven't you?' he addressed her harshly. 'What have you come up here to do now?'

She looked at him with green, defiant eyes.

'You seem to forget, Shane, we are engaged and that we were to have been married four days ago. You backed out of it with this—this woman—and the whole of Johannesburg is laughing at me. A gallant thing for you to have done, isn't it?'

'More gallant than the thing you did when you went to Jalessa and lied to Evelyn,' he retorted.

'I don't care. All's fair in love and war. You say you love her, but I love you—so we're quits.'

'Love doesn't do such contemptible things,' he said. 'Go back to England and forget that we were to have been married, because I shall never marry you, knowing what I do now.'

'Oh—won't you!' Vicky bit hard on her red lips, and her brilliant jade eyes glittered through their long lashes. She swung round to Veriland. 'Are you going to stand there and see me jilted—because my fiancé wants *your wife*?'

Veriland came forward in his blustering way.

'No—certainly not. See here, Cargill. If Evelyn is coming back to me, then you must go back to Miss Sinclair and carry out your contract with her.'

'No—I'm hanged if I do,' said Shane furiously.

Evelyn put a hand to her throat. She felt physically ill, sick to the heart with the whole thing. Her head was burning. How terribly, indeed, had Gordon's coming destroyed the peace of Mountain Lodge. She thought drearily:

'There are times when I feel I can't stand any more pain or grief; when I wish Shane and I were dead, buried together up here in the mountains, and that it was all finished.'

She heard Gordon's harsh voice:

'You must change your mind, Cargill. Either you shall go through with your marriage with Miss Sinclair or this cable must be sent.'

'Oh, no—not that!' burst from Evelyn despairingly.

Shane put a hand to his head. Heavens, was he to be driven and forced like this—as well as Evelyn? It was intolerable. For a moment he could not think straight; could not speak. His brain was whirling.

Veriland eyed Vicky uneasily. There was a nasty look on her face when she looked at him. He knew that she held his secret; she was well aware that Charles Mayton was dead. He didn't wish her to impart that news to Evelyn. Therefore he must help her to get what *she* wanted, and she seemed determined to marry Shane.

'You take Miss Sinclair back to Johannesburg and marry her, Cargill,' said Gordon Veriland. 'It's the only thing to do—under the circumstances. Otherwise—that cable goes to my lawyers. Of course, if you don't mind whether Evelyn's father gets seven years or not——' he finished with a shrug of the shoulders.

Shane doubled his fists. With all his heart he longed to smash Veriland's face to pulp. Then he looked at Evelyn and his temper cooled. The poor darling, with her great beseeching grey eyes and quivering lips. She was suffering agonies. He knew it. She was so tender-hearted. She'd never be able to bear the thought of her father in gaol, year after year. He'd spare her that agony if he could. He wouldn't be the cause of that cablegram going to England. No, what the hell did it matter now whether he married his cousin or not? He'd never live with her—he'd see to that. He hated the sight of her. But since he was saying good-bye to Evelyn to-day and to all hope of happiness, which would go with her, nothing else mattered at all.

'Very well,' he said shortly. 'I'll carry out my contract with Vicky. But I have a condition to impose, Veriland. That this is the last time you use Evelyn's father as a weapon to coerce either her or me into doing anything. Is that a bet? If you do it again, then, by God, I swear I'll put a bullet through you and swing for it—gladly.'

Veriland turned livid. He licked his lips.

'I—swear I—won't coerce Evelyn or you through her father—ever again,' he muttered.

'Good,' said Shane. He turned to Evelyn; took her hands and kissed them each in turn. 'Good-bye, my dearest. God bless you and help you. If you're going to be unhappy, so am I. My marriage will mean nothing to me—you know that.'

'Thanks,' said Vicky furiously, tapping her foot on the ground. But mixed with her anger, her bitter jealousy of Evelyn, was triumph. She'd got Shane; got him cold. And later—when he was her husband—she'd make him understand that she wasn't going to be neglected for a dozen Evelyns.

Evelyn gave her lover one last, long look.

'It doesn't seem fair—that you should be made to suffer because of my father,' she whispered brokenly.

'My marriage will mean no more to me than yours does to you,' he said. 'I love only you.'

'And I—you.'

124

'Come along, Evelyn,' said Veriland angrily.

She turned and went with him, blindly. Shane looked after the slim, lovely figure; the fair, drooping head. Then he turned to his cousin.

'Do you want me to marry you—knowing that I dislike and despise you?' he asked bluntly.

She flushed.

'Yes, I do,' she said defiantly.

'Very well,' said Shane, his eyes very blue and grim. 'Then I wish you joy of it.'

But Vicky was thinking:

'This mood will pass. I'll make him change his tune. I'm attractive, and when I'm his wife—we'll see!'

They drove back to Johannesburg in silence. Shane felt ice-cold and grimmer than he had ever been in his life. He had been forced into saying he would marry Vicky, but his one wish was to be alone with his memories of Evelyn. He wondered that any woman should want him on such terms as Vicky had got him. How he despised her!—her treachery; her cruelty; her utter selfishness!

He felt almost horrified at the thought that she had grown into such a creature. In their youth, at home, he had been fond of her, and in later years she had seemed a good friend; a relative to be proud of—beautiful, smart, amusing. But now—

He could not shut his mind to the picture of Evelyn's pale, tragic face and the thought of her submitting to Gordon Veriland's caresses.

'Oh, God!' he said, and did not know that he spoke aloud.

Vicky glanced at him uneasily, stopped her car, which she had been driving, and put a hand over his clenched one.

'Shane—don't take it so hard. Try and forget

125

that woman. I am sincerely in love with you. If I've been cruel and lied to you and betrayed you—it's because I wanted you so badly. Can't you understand—when you, yourself, are in love?'

He looked at her coldly, drawing his hand from hers.

'No matter how much I cared for Evelyn, I would never have ruined other people's happiness as you have ruined mine.'

'It's not me so much as Gordon Veriland,' she muttered, trying to excuse herself.

'You've done harm enough.'

'Well, as we're going to get married, let's be pleasant to each other.'

'You know why I'm marrying you. Under protest,' he reminded her harshly. 'Don't demand anything from me, Vicky, because you won't get it.'

'You can't be so heartless, Shane. After all, you ran away on our wedding-eve—it was frightfully cruel to me!' Vicky's voice broke. Tears of passion glittered in her eyes. She wreathed her arms about Shane's neck, took off her hat, and nestled her beautiful red head against his shoulder. 'Shane, kiss me—make friends with me again.'

He did not move. His lips were a thin, forbidding line. She kissed them and they remained closed and cold. She embraced him passionately. His arms remained fixed at his sides. He did not move or yield a fraction. But when she looked at him flushed, resentful, in tears, he gave her a freezing smile.

'Did you enjoy that? Will you like being married to me—under protest?'

Vicky felt almost murderous; but she bit fiercely at her lips, dashed away her tears, and said:

'Yes, I don't care—I *will* marry you.'

'Very well—let's get on,' he almost snarled at her.

She drove on—injured, angry, vowing to win him in the end. He sat silent, staring blindly ahead of him and thinking:

'Eve—Eve—my Sweet—shall I ever, ever see you again in this world?'

XVII

Evelyn returned to the hotel with her husband and went straight to her bedroom and locked herself in. When Gordon fumed and fussed outside and demanded an entry, she answered:

'Not to-night. I must be alone to-night. To-morrow—as you wish—but I insist upon being alone now.'

He had no choice but to give in to her.

Evelyn unlocked her door only to the waiters who brought her food.

For the rest of that day and night she sat alone, crouched in a chair by the window, staring out at the hard blue sky that blazed over Johannesburg, and wishing that she had died up in Mountain Lodge while she was still in Shane's arms, with his lips upon her mouth.

She had lost him—for ever. Not lost his love; no, she would never lose that, she knew it. She had implicit faith in him now. But she had lost the tangible Shane; the dear, brown-faced, blue-eyed Shane; the gay, passionate, perfect lover. Doubly lost him. She had returned to Gordon and *he* was to marry Vicky. She was no longer jealous of Vicky, but the idea rankled. It was so cruel; that Vicky should become Mrs. Shane Cargill when she, Evelyn, would have given half her life to bear that precious name.

She thought, in the bitter, lonely hours of that day and night, of her father. She pictured him cruising through the Mediterranean. It was a long while since she heard from him. When would he write again? It would be good to hear that he was well and happy and to know that her terrific sacrifice was not in vain.

Each time Gordon called outside her door she shuddered and thought:

'To-morrow I will have to give way to him.'

When night came, she undressed, lay in bed and stared out at the starry sky with dry, aching eyes, and wondered how long her endurance would stand the strain.

She thought of her lover and remembered, with bitter-sweet passion, every kiss, every caress that they had exchanged; every lovely moment of intimacy that there had been between them.

She thought:

'I *lived* when I was with you, beloved. Without you—I shall be a dead thing.'

She thought too, that it was some consolation to her to know how indisputably he loved her. He had sacrificed himself to Vicky for her sake—to spare her suffering over her father. All her life she would be grateful to him for that.

Morning came. Evelyn was not a coward. She must face all the cruelty and difficulties of life as Gordon Veriland's wife, and she knew it. She joined him after breakfast in the hotel lounge and tried to behave as though nothing had happened; she wished to appear submissive, calm, and resigned as she had been after Jalessa.

Veriland handed her a local paper.

'See that,' he said, pointing to a paragraph.

She looked at it dully. For a moment her pale cheeks flushed with hot colour and her eyes dilated as though with pain; then she handed the paper back to her husband.

'Yes,' she said quietly.

Vicky had wasted no time. That paragraph stated that the wedding of Miss Victoria Sinclair and Mr. Shane Cargill, which had been postponed owing to the 'illness of the bridegroom,' would take place to-morrow at the registrar's at half-past eleven, after which the 'happy couple' expected to leave for Cape Town and England for the honeymoon.

'You see, you needn't waste time thinking about Cargill any more,' said Gordon Veriland, eyeing his wife slyly. 'He's going to fix it up with his cousin and quit South Africa.'

'Yes,' said Evelyn in the same quiet voice. 'I see.'

He took her arm in a possessive way.

'Come, come, Evelyn—don't look like this. You married me and you might as well make the best of it.'

'Yes,' she said without any feeling.

'What do you want? I'll buy you anything you want.'

'I only want peace,' she said with more passion. 'Your money can't buy that.'

'Oh, hell!' he said savagely. 'Buck up, for heaven's sake, and be a bit more amusing. Now, look here—this is our last night in this town. To-morrow we'll move off and travel—we'll do Algiers and Egypt and the South of France if you like.'

'I'd like to see Daddy,' she said wistfully. 'You said, while I was ill in Jalessa, that you heard he was going to travel in the Mediterranean. Perhaps by the time we get to France he will have gone home. Let's go to London and see him.'

Veriland made no reply. He scowled at the ground. The last thing he wanted to do was to go to London—where his young wife would immediately discover that her father was dead.

'Yes, yes, we'll fix something,' he said.

'I'm going to write to Daddy now,' said Evelyn.

Veriland watched her walk into the writing-room. This business was getting on his nerves. He would have to be very careful about Evelyn and her father. Whatever happened, she must not find out that he was dead.

He was watching the mail very carefully. He had given orders, wherever they stayed, that all letters were to be taken to him, in case anyone from home gave Evelyn the information he desired to keep from her.

That night he insisted that she should put on a pretty dress and go out with him to dinner and a theatre. She sat through the show, a pale, silent figure, her sorrowful eyes fixed on the stage; but her mind was concentrated upon her lover. She thought:

'Where is he? What is he doing to-night? To-morrow he will be married and leaving Johannesburg with Vicky.'

The idea hurt, horribly, despite all her efforts to abstract her attention from it and stamp it out.

Gordon bought her flowers; gave her a new jewel —a diamond brooch worth hundreds of pounds, which had been put in a little red case on her plate at dinner-time. She accepted the jewel coldly and without gratitude. She did not want it. She loathed her husband and his presents. But because he demanded it, she wore the brooch and the flowers.

Veriland was maddened by her coldness.

'Can't you thaw for one second—you little icicle?' he asked, when they were in their car, driving back to the hotel from the theatre. He had caught her fiercely in his arms and put his lips to her shoulder. 'You belong to me, Evelyn. I can be as good a lover as Cargill—if you'll let me—darling.'

She shuddered and closed her eyes, every nerve in her slender body jarred and quivering. She felt Gordon's hot lips against hers and cried, inwardly:

'Shane, Shane—there can be no lover for me— but you!'

'Kiss me,' said Gordon impatiently.

'No,' she gasped. 'No—I can't. You've forced me to come back to you—but I can't kiss you—I can't make myself love you—because I despise you—*hate you*—for what you have done to all of us.'

'Very well,' he muttered. 'Hate me—despise me—I don't care. I'm your husband, and if you won't kiss me, I must be content with kissing you.'

His arms, his lips, claimed her, hurt her, destroyed her. She was helpless and hopeless, and that night was another shameful, bitter, intolerable memory to be added to the rest.

XVIII

Early that next day, the day which was to mark Shane's wedding with Vicky Sinclair, Evelyn rose, dressed, and went out for a long walk. She felt exhausted and miserable. She wanted to be alone, and early morning was the coolest, nicest part of the South African day.

She felt better after the long walk and returned

to the hotel. She was told that Mr. Veriland had breakfasted and had gone out on business. He left a message for her that he would be back soon after eleven.

At a quarter past eleven the second mail came in, and a page brought Evelyn a letter. Unluckily for Veriland's plans, that letter was addressed to Mrs. Gordon Veriland and was edged with black. Evelyn opened it, perplexed by the band of mourning. She knew the writing. It was an old servant—a faithful cook who had been with her father and mother for many years and known her since she was a baby.

When Evelyn saw the contents of that letter she went pale to the lips and her heart thudded violently. She sat staring at it—reading it again and again.

'When I saw the news of your Dear Father's death in the *Times*, I felt, Miss Evelyn, I must rite to you as you have bin so kind to me.'

'*Your Dear Father's death.*' That sentence in the kindly old cook's uneducated handwriting danced in front of the girl's vision. *Father's death*. In the *Times*. What date was this? It was a month old. Her father must have died—a month ago.

Evelyn's throat felt dry. A pulse beat madly there. An agonising lump. Father was dead— poor, poor Daddy! He had died a month ago. Why hadn't she heard? Where had he died? *Did Gordon know?*

She looked at the other letters. Then she saw one addressed to Gordon Veriland, Esq., in a familiar writing. She recognised it—the writing of old Forbes, her father's lawyer. In a frenzy, Evelyn ripped open this letter. She read only the first few lines:

'Dear Veriland.

'I understand your wife is too ill to attend to any legal matters attached to the winding up of her father's estate, so I am sending you various documents for signature if she will kindly give you power of attorney——'

With burning eyes and shaking hands, Evelyn sprang to her feet. So Gordon had known for weeks, perhaps months, and had been in communication with her father's lawyers behind her back.

She understood now why she had not heard from Daddy. That tale about the Mediterranean cruise had been fiction. Gordon must have known about Daddy while they were in Jalessa. He had kept it from her in order to exercise his power over her. How monstrous! How abominable of him!

Gordon Veriland came into the hotel. He approached his wife, smiling, but the smile died when he saw her face and the letters in her hand. Good heavens, what had happened? What had she found out? Damn it, he had expected to be back in time to get that mail.

Evelyn wasted no time.

'I know everything,' she said between clenched teeth. 'I know that Daddy is dead. And you kept it from me—*kept it back*—you cur!'

'Now, come, Evelyn.' He was scarlet and stuttering, dumbfounded because she had found him out. 'I did it for the best. You were ill——'

'It wasn't that!' she broke in. 'It was to keep me from Shane. Yes, to keep me from the man I love.

But you won't do that any more. I shall go to him now—now, I say!'

She broke off hysterically, turned and rushed to the door. Veriland followed.

'You can't do this. You've got to stay with me. You're my wife.'

She swung round on him, blazing-eyed; the icicle thawing to a furious rage and indignation for the trick practised upon her.

'I was your wife only for Daddy's sake. Now he is gone beyond your mean vengeance, I'm free to join my lover.'

'But you forget,' said Veriland harshly, 'that he isn't free. He was married to Vicky—*exactly ten minutes ago.*'

Evelyn looked at the clock in the vestibule of the hotel. She saw it as through a mist. *Twenty-five minutes past eleven.* This morning's paper had announced that Shane and Vicky were being married at a quarter past. She was ten minutes too late.

She went white and a deathly feeling came into her heart. It couldn't be true that Shane was married to Vicky now, when he need not do it, when he need not keep away from her, Evelyn; when they were free, at last, to go together to the very ends of the earth and would hurt nobody by doing so! Only for Charles Mayton's sake had they suffered and parted and made such sacrifices.

Evelyn nearly went mad. She looked at her husband with blazing eyes of hatred. Never in her life had she hated anybody as she hated this man who was the cause of all the heartbreak and tragedy.

'You won't stop me from going to Shane,' she said between her teeth, shaking from head to foot. 'Nothing you can say or do will stop me. They may be late at the registrar's. I may stop the marriage yet. I shall try, anyhow. I shall do everything on earth to stop Shane from sacrificing himself to that vile woman—now that I know poor Daddy is dead!'

'Look here,' began Veriland, stuttering.

But the slim young figure turned and darted out of the hotel into the brilliant sunshine. He followed, red in the face, cursing his luck. He had no hold over her now. He knew it. Damn that old busybody of a cook—writing to Evelyn. Damn the page for delivering the letter to her instead of to him. All his plans would fail—if by any chance Evelyn got to the registry office in time to stop Shane's wedding.

He had better follow Evelyn, whatever happened. He would not count her as lost until he actually saw her depart with her lover. An unquenchable flame of desire for her still burned furiously in Gordon Veriland—desire for her slender, delicate body; her pale gold hair; her wide grey eyes so exquisitely set between the black, silky lashes. Not easily would he see her go with Shane Cargill.

Evelyn sat in a hired car and was driven at a reckless pace through the busy thoroughfares of Johannesburg to the registry office.

'Treble your fare if you get me there in time,' she had told the driver.

She sat forward on the seat, her trembling fingers scarcely able to hold the bag she was carrying. Her eyes stared blindly ahead of her. Her mind whirled with a constant revolution of chaotic thought.

Daddy was dead. *Daddy was dead.* Gordon had kept the news back in a most abominable fashion. He had kept her in ignorance, knowing that it was his one and only hold over her. Oh, what infamy on his part! Despairingly she looked back and recalled all the anguish that she might have been spared if she had known poor Daddy had died. Her grief for him was poignant and acute enough, but she was a woman—passionately in love—and it was only natural that her first thought was for her lover.

There was nothing on earth now to prevent her from walking out of the house of the man who had forced her to marry him—from going to Shane—staying with him. She did not care whether Gordon divorced her or not. Shane would not care either. They adored each other. They had been made each for the other. Life apart was intolerable.

If only she had known last night—or even earlier in the day. What would she do if she found that Shane had made Vicky his wife? Well—even then she would tell him the truth and perhaps the marriage could be made null and void. She knew that Vicky had behaved vilely, did not deserve to have Shane as her husband. Evelyn felt no compunction in doing her level best to stop that marriage, now.

Of course there was a traffic jam; they were hung up in it for ten minutes. To Evelyn it seemed like ten hours. In an agony of impatience she sat waiting for the policeman to give the signal for them to pass through. She bit so fiercely at her lip that when she pressed her handkerchief to it, she found it flecked with blood.

At last they were at the registry office. Evelyn told the driver to wait. She rushed in, every nerve in her body pulsating, throbbing, hurting.

Was Shane there?

Only one person was there; a little bald-headed man with gold-rimmed spectacles, peering over a big ledger. A clerk.

'Mr. Cargill'—Evelyn literally gasped the name—'has Mr. Cargill been here?'

The little man peered at her kindly.

'Why, yes, madam. Mr. Cargill and Miss Sinclair were married here just a few minutes ago.'

Evelyn swayed on her feet and put a hand to her eyes. The clerk, much concerned, jumped up and ran to her side.

'Are you ill, madam?'

'No,' she whispered, and recovered herself and added: 'Where have they gone—do you—know?'

'I believe the happy couple left by train for Cape Town, madam. They were catching the s.s. *Rhodesian Castle* for England.'

Evelyn stared stonily in front of her. Her heart was gripped by a frightful feeling of despair. But despair was mixed with a frantic and passionate belief that even not she must get to Shane and tell him the truth and stop him from leaving South Africa.

She rushed wildly from the registry office, leaving a bewildered clerk to stare after her. Her eyes were suffused; her cheeks ashen. She did not see the crowded streets. She was like one demented. The only human being she had ever really adored, and who was so much part of her, had been unjustly torn from her side and had united himself to another woman, and it was too much to be borne. She said to the taxi-driver:

'The station quickly!'

Within half an hour she was a passenger in the second boat-train to Cape Town. The first one had already departed with the 'happy couple' in it. Happy couple. Ironic words. Evelyn crouched in a corner of a first-class carriage and stared blindly out of the window and wondered if Shane was as unhappy as she had been before the news of her father's death had reached her now. She was more than unhappy now. Desperate—crazy—filled with only one great overwhelming desire. To get to her lover and tell him everything before it was too late.

It seemed to her that hours passed instead of minutes; days instead of hours. Rushing across the hot, sunlit country to the coast, she kept repeating her lover's name.

'Shane—Shane—Shane!'

She was trembling and nerve-racked when she reached Cape Town and drove to the docks.

Was she in time? What time did the boat sail? She *must* see Shane. She knew that he was only taking Vicky to England because he despaired of seeing her again. She knew that when he heard about her father's death he would at once return to her and never leave her again.

Like one in a nightmare, she found herself on the docks, amidst a motley crowd of sailors—Dutch, African, European. All about her was the noise of working cranes, lifting great bales of goods, the shrill sound of sirens hooting, deafening her. She saw a little crowd of white people—well-dressed men and women—waving handkerchiefs, small flags, scarves. At what were they waving? At a big white liner moving majestically out from shore over the intensely blue, rippling sea.

Through bloodshot eyes Evelyn regarded this great boat. She clutched the arm of a sailor passing her.

'What liner is that?'

'*Rhodesian Castle*,' he said, and moved on.

Rhodesian Castle. The name burnt into Evelyn's brain. The boat which was bearing Shane and his wife away from South Africa, and hundreds of miles away—to England.

She was too late. The ship had sailed. It was in sight; but it had sailed. She could just see a group of people on deck; tiny figures in the distance, waving to those on the docks. Shane, perhaps, was amongst them—bidding a silent farewell to her, Evelyn.

It was more than she could endure. A red-hot wave of agony surged over her. She could not let him go; could not lose him like this. Once he got away with Vicky he would be utterly lost to her. She knew it. She screamed aloud:

'Shane! SHANE!'

Nobody heard her; nobody noticed the frantic young figure, the ghastly young face.

Then Evelyn ran forward, propelled by something stronger than herself. Ran and flung herself into the sunlit, sapphire water. She would follow, swim to the ship, reach her lover somehow.

A splash, a few bubbles, then a wet golden head appearing on the surface of the water. After that, chaos. Two Dutch sailors, working on the dock, saw and dived in after the white-clad figure which was striking out, frantically, to sea.

There was a roaring in Evelyn's ears; a choking in her throat; the sun blinded her. She felt hands clutch her and pull her back. She screamed desperately:

'No—no! Oh, Shane—*Shane!*'

And after that, oblivion, a merciful blotting out of the agony.

A crowd gathered round the slim, dripping figure which was laid gently on the dock. An accident or suicide? Who knew? How beautiful she was; marble-pale; gold hair wet, plastered down on the lovely head; long black lashes veiling the big eyes.

A man fought his way through the crowd. A big, fair Englishman with a hot, perspiring face. Gordon Veriland had followed and seen his wife fling herself into the harbour. Aghast—not because he had driven her to such lengths, but because he was afraid he might lose her altogether—he hastened to her side.

'She is my wife,' he said. 'Get a rug—something to wrap her in—a car—quickly.'

When Evelyn recovered consciousness she found herself in bed in a big hotel in Cape Town, with a hospital nurse and doctor in attendance and her husband seated by her side.

She sat up, wildly, fighting for breath.

'Shane—Shane,' she panted.

'It's all right, my dear—you're safe and sound with me. I'll look after you,' said Veriland, leaning over her.

She looked up at him with her tragic eyes and fell back on the pillow. Realisation returned to her and stunned her. Shane had sailed and she had failed to reach him. She was in Gordon's hands again. She felt incapable of fighting him again. But as soon as Gordon was out of the room she asked the nurse for a pencil and paper.

'I want you to send a wireless—at once,' she panted. 'And on no condition must you show it to—Mr. Veriland. Please take it out yourself, to the post-office, *now*.'

XIX

On board the s.s. *Rhodesian Castle* Shane Cargill leaned over the rails and stared wretchedly at the sea. It was dark; he could see nothing but the moonlit, rippling water through which the big liner ploughed its way homewards, and the twinkling phosphorous just below him. For an hour or more he had been watching the shore fade from sight, saying good-bye not only to South Africa but to all that he most loved and held dear.

It was frightful to him to contemplate that Evelyn—his darling—was still in Johannesburg, a victim to Gordon Veriland. Frightful to think that he was totally separated from her now. There had been no more unhappy man in Africa than Shane Cargill when he had married Victoria Sinclair in the Johannesburg registry office this morning. It had been as much as he could do to force himself to say the necessary word and put the ring on Vicky's finger. He hated Vicky and all that she stood for. Treachery, blackmail, his own bondage, Evelyn's martyrdom.

But he believed that he had done the right thing for Evelyn. He had helped to save her father and therefore ensured her peace of mind. And, of course, he had made it plain to Vicky that she was his wife in name only. Never would he touch her. Never would he hold any woman in his arms again. Evelyn was the last.

He thought it best to clear out of South Africa—avoid it like the plague—and so get away from temptation—the temptation of going back to Eve.

He would settle down in England. He was rich. Vicky could spend his money—do as she wished. He did not care—so long as she left him alone.

He heard the boom of a gong. That meant he must dress for dinner. He wanted a drink. By God, yes—plenty of drink—something to make him forget. He would go crazy if he stayed up here on deck, staring at the sea and wanting Evelyn.

He met his wife as he turned into the saloon. His wife! He resented the fact that she had a legal right to that name. She greeted him cheerily, as though they were the best of friends.

'Hullo, Shane.'

He did not answer. She looked delightful—all in white—a cream sweater and pleated skirt—her beautiful red hair bare, her eyes sparkling in the moonlight. But he was blind to her physical charms.

'Shane, you've neglected your bride terribly,' she murmured, taking his arm. 'Come and talk to me while I change for dinner.'

'Sorry,' he said icily, drawing his arm away, 'but I'm going to the bar.'

He walked straight past her—his brown, handsome face as hard as flint.

Vicky narrowed her green eyes and gazed resentfully after him. So he was determined to be nasty—to grieve over that little beast of an Evelyn—to give her, his wife, the cold shoulder. Going to the bar, was he? Vicky pursed her lips. H'm. Well, let him go. Let him get tight. It might do him good and make him more amenable.

Vicky meant to seduce her own husband before the voyage was over. She wasn't going to be cold-shouldered. Neither did she intend that he should waste the time fretting about another woman.

While Shane, with a lot of other men in the bar, drank many more cocktails than were good for him, and strove desperately to efface the memory of Evelyn, Vicky changed for dinner.

She had a luxurious state-cabin—Shane was in the one next to her. She whistled a tune as she bathed; perfumed herself lavishly and put on her most alluring dress; black chiffon; sheer black silk stockings; black marocain shoes with high jewelled heels. She looked well in black Her skin was so white; wonderful with that blazing red hair.

Vicky looked at herself in the mirror and touched her voluptuous mouth with red salve.

'Not an unattractive bride, are you, my dear?' she said to her reflection. 'You ought to be able to light a flame in your husband—if he's flesh and blood. And methinks Shane is very human!'

Somebody knocked at the door.

'Come in,' said Vicky airily.

A steward entered.

'Wireless for Mr. Cargill.'

'Give it to me—he's not here at the moment,' said Vicky.

The steward gave her the wireless and departed. Vicky lit a cigarette, put it between her red lips, and coolly opened the envelope. She was not going to allow her husband to have secrets from her. Who was the wireless from? Congratulations from a pal, perhaps.

Then, when Vicky read that message, the cigarette dropped from her lips. She crushed it with her heel. Her green eyes narrowed until they were like a cat's; mere slits.

'Tried to reach you in time and failed stop am at Queen's Hotel Cape Town ill in bed stop come to me at once stop I have found out my father is dead and we need not make this sacrifice oh come quickly Eve.'

Vicky was white under the rouge when she had read and digested that message. What an awful business. Evelyn knew the truth. How had she found out? That blundering fool, Gordon. He'd

143

made a mess of it. Savagely Vicky crumpled the wireless in her hand. She breathed quickly. If Shane got that message—that frantic appeal—he would land at the next port and go straight back to Evelyn. She knew it. She knew he would have given a lot to hear that Charles Mayton was dead.

However, it was a bit of luck that the wireless was delivered to her. *Why should Shane see it?* No reason at all. And why shouldn't she answer it? She could think of something that would put an end to Evelyn's attempts to get Shane back.

Vicky speedily made up her mind. She was madly in love with her husband. He was married to her now, and she was absolutely determined to make him her lover—to-night—so that there should be no drawing back for him.

She would establish a more intimate and binding tie than the legal one of marriage. She would have a child. Yes, if she bore Shane a child, he would not leave her.

Vicky's nostrils dilated. She rang the bell. A stewardess appeared. Vicky handed her a sheet of paper.

'Take that to the wireless operator and have it sent off at once,' she said.

'Yes, madam,' said the woman, and retired.

So a wireless message flashed its way across the sea to Cape Town and was delivered to Mrs. Gordon Veriland at the Queen's Hotel early that morning.

Evelyn read the wireless with a heart nearly bursting with grief and pain and a sense of complete disaster.

'Received yours and regret terribly too late stop I am married to Vicky and must do my duty

144

by her now stop we must never meet again stop good-bye and help me to do my duty by doing yours Shane.'

Again and again Evelyn read that message—read it until the blinding, scalding tears began to pour down her white little face and great aching sobs choked her throat. It was too late. Shane would not come back. She was bitterly disappointed. She had felt so sure he would come. But Vicky had been cunning in her wording of that message; made it kind and regretful; appealed to Evelyn 'to help him' by doing her own duty. She had known that would appeal to Evelyn. And Evelyn never doubted that Shane had written those words.

Very well. She must face the tragic fact now that he was lost to her for ever. He was going to stand by Vicky. Well, she would not try to prevent him from doing as he wished. But on one point she was adamant. She would not stay with Gordon. Nothing would induce her to. She would leave him and get work in Johannesburg; earn her own living; do anything rather than stay with him after the dreadful things he had done to her.

But she thought:

'Oh, Shane, Shane—I was so certain you would come to me when you knew—Shane, how can I bear this pain?'

Perhaps she loved him more than he loved her.

Yet, had she but known it, he, who would have flung away his entire fortune for the sake of getting that wireless message which Vicky had intercepted, drank himself into a state of semi-intoxication on board the *Rhodesian Castle*, and was the most miserable man in the world.

If only he could forget Evelyn—forget that thrilling, satisfying, glorious love which had existed between them! He went on drinking steadily until the gong boomed for dinner. He passed from a stage of misery to one of indifference to his fate. Damn everybody—everything—what did he care? What did anything matter?

With his finer instincts somewhat blurred, and a tormented look in his fine blue eyes, Shane Cargill went down to his cabin. He muttered to himself:

'To hell with it all. What does anything matter?'

He saw the world through a slight haze. When he entered his cabin he found Vicky waiting for him. Vicky, looking amazingly lovely in the long black chiffon dress which clung tightly to her magnificent figure. Shane's eyes travelled over her, from the red hair to the slim black-slippered feet.

'Nice ankles—pretty woman!' he said, and laughed a trifle stupidly.

Vicky stood up. She was cool, watchful, well aware that Shane was not sober. But her heart leapt as she saw what lay in his eyes. A look not good to see—but it was exactly what *she* wanted.

She walked straight up to him and put her bare white arms about his neck.

'I've been waiting for you, darling—hours,' she whispered.

He looked at her, his nostrils dilating a little. He said thickly:

'Get out—don't care a damn—for you.'

'Oh, yes, you do. I'm your wife. This is our wedding night. Shane—and you do care about me.'

'Go to hell,' he said, and laughed.

Vicky leaned against him and pulled his dark, handsome head down to hers.

'Yes—gladly—if you'll come with me. Shane, I love you. I belong to you. Aren't you going to kiss—your wife?'

For a moment he did not speak, did not move. He only saw her white, upturned face, with its red, sensuous mouth, as through a haze. The perfume of her red hair mounted to his head. He wanted to push her away, to be left alone, to go to sleep. He didn't want any dinner; any women; anything.

Vicky clung closer. He felt her lips against his; hotly; passionately. His senses whirled, drowned in the sheer passion of the moment.

'You red-haired devil,' he said, and kissed her violently, bruising her mouth.

Vicky, triumphant, exalting in this seduction of her own husband, gave a little cry.

'Oh—darling!'

He felt himself drowning in the tempestuous perfume of her embrace. His last feeling was: *'What does anything matter?'* Then he kissed her white shoulder through the thin black chiffon of her frock. Both his arms went round her.

'Devil,' he muttered again, and laughed.

She clung to him deliriously; reached out a hand and switched off the cabin light.

Mr. and Mrs. Shane Cargill did not appear in the dining-saloon that night. Shane Cargill slept—in a drunken stupor—in the white, treacherous arms of his wife, the woman he had sworn never to touch. His heart would be broken if he had known that in tiny pieces in the waste-paper basket in that cabin lay a wireless message from Evelyn; a desperate appeal which, had he read it, would have sent him speeding back to her and saved him from abandonment that night.

In the morning, Shane, sober again, with a splitting head and a feeling of nausea, paced the sunlit deck. He let the fresh salt wind blow against his face and loathed both Vicky and himself.

Sick at heart, utterly disgusted with himself, he wondered how he could have done what he did. Fool to have drunk too much; fool to have succumbed to the lure of a woman who had helped to hurt Evelyn so badly. He was terribly ashamed, and regretful, and he felt unutterably disloyal to the memory of the woman he loved.

Vicky had triumphed last night—but this morning she found herself up against a stone wall. Shane avoided her and refused to discuss what had happened to her.

'I apologise,' he had said, before he left the cabin. 'I was not responsible for what I did. But it will never occur again.'

When she had protested that she adored him and wanted him, he had cut her short.

'We agreed that we should not live together. That ends it,' he said.

Vicky did not argue. Sullenly she accepted defeat. But she had triumphed once, and she meant to be the victor again. Whatever happened, she always had her wedding night to remember and bring up against him.

For the rest of that voyage Shane barely spoke to his wife and could not look at her without hating himself for that one night of weakness and surrender.

Half the night, most of the day, he concentrated on the thought of Evelyn. Between Vicky and himself there had been intoxication, passion, mere sensuousness. But between Eve and himself love had been sublimated—had meant tenderness—respect —as well as passion. He was broken-hearted every time his thought dwelt on the sweet memory of Eve.

He thought of Dowson's famous poem 'Cynara.' It found an echo in his own soul:

*'I have flung roses riotously with the throng,
Dancing to put thy pale lost lilies out of mind—
I cried for madder music and for stronger wine;
But when the feast is finished and the lamps expire,
Then falls the shadow, Cynara, and the night is thine!'*

He substituted the name Evelyn for Cynara, and repeated that verse to himself again and again.

Never, never could he put her pale lost lilies out of mind. Her shadow fell incessantly before him.

Nothing would induce him to soften toward Vicky again during the rest of the voyage. One night he even insulted her when she came, in her dressing-gown, to his cabin and tried to stir him to passion for her. He turned her out, brutally. But Vicky had no pride. She was furious—malicious—and she meant to win him yet.

Unfortunately for her plans she made one false move. She forgot to pay, personally, for that wireless which she had sent to Evelyn Veriland.

Shane, examining his bill at the end of the voyage, on the morning of the day they landed at Southampton, noticed a small amount for a wireless. He strolled along to the wireless operator's cabin.

'Isn't this a mistake?' he asked the operator, smiling.

The man looked at his ledger.

'No, sir. That's right. It was sent off by Mrs. Cargill on the first day we put out from Cape Town. In answer to the one that came for you.'

'One that came for me?' repeated Shane, pricking up his ears.

'Yes, sir. On the same day. I sent it to you.'

'I did not get it,' said Shane sharply. 'Have you a copy?'

'Yes, sir. We keep duplicates.'

The operator found the duplicate and handed it to Shane. When he read that desperate and feverish message from the woman he loved, his heart seemed to stop beating—then rush on at a terrific pace. *Good God*—Evelyn's father was dead. He need not have married Vicky; he need never have left South Africa and Evelyn. And she had wired for him, begged him to go to her. Vicky had known—had intercepted the message; kept it from him.

His face was ashen when he realised the frightfulness of this thing. While Evelyn waited for him, wanted him, needed him, and nothing existed to keep them apart, he had drunk himself half insane and surrendered to the physical lure of a thoroughly wicked woman.

Shane nearly went mad.

He rushed down to his wife's cabin and found her. He was furious-eyed, bitter-tongued.

'You rotten little traitress,' he snarled at her. 'I think you're the vilest woman I've ever known in my life.'

Vicky quailed. So he had found out about that wireless from Evelyn. What a disaster!

'How dared you do it?' he said. He seized her wrist and hung over her, his face ashen. 'How dared you keep my wireless from me and send that lying message back to *her*? Do you think you've gained anything by it? Nothing. You've only kept me from Evelyn six weeks longer than was necessary. I'm going back to Cape Town on the next boat—to-day if I can find one sailing from Southampton; and when I get back, I shall never leave Evelyn again in this life!'

XX

Vicky, for the first time in her life, was at a loss for words or action. Under the bitter lash of her husband's words she shrank, white and trembling, one hand to her lips, her eyes wide and frightened. When he turned his back on her, she called after him hoarsely:

'Shane—no—don't leave me like this—you can't!'

He swung round on her, laughing harshly.

' Oh—can't I? Watch me! I can leave you easily. I never wanted to marry you—you know it. I did it to save Evelyn's father. I told you the facts. You chose to marry me in spite of it. You blackmailed me into it—you and Gordon Veriland between you. And no doubt you knew, as well as Veriland, that Mayton died months ago. You're a rotten, vile couple—rotten to the core—the pair of you. I owe you nothing and I have no compunction whatsoever in leaving you—now.'

He marched into his own cabin. Vicky followed, her face tinged with grey, her tall, lissom figure shaking. Bad though she was, she was crazily in love with this man—as much in love as Vicky could be, which was a physical rather than a mental thing. She was aghast at the thought of losing him.

'Shane—I'm sorry if I—if I've behaved rottenly,' she began to stammer. 'Don't be too hard on me, Shane. I loved you—honestly——'

He did not take the slightest notice of her. He

busied himself about the cabin, packing the remainder of his things. From above came the clatter of feet on deck, the sound of bells, sirens hooting. The *Rhodesian Castle* was nearing Southampton Harbour. The long voyage from Cape Town was at an end. Through the porthole came the grey light of a typically English morning in May. Warmish, misty, cold to the South Africans.

Shane's whole mind was concentrated upon Evelyn. He must send her a cable. Better send it to the Queen's, Cape Town, the place from which she had cabled him. Oh, God, how unfortunate for them all that that cable had not been delivered, personally, into his hands! What a frightful stroke of misfortune that it should have been withheld from him by this vile, unscrupulous girl whom he had married. He resented, fiercely, the family tie between them; the fact that she was his second cousin; and most of all that she was his wife.

But never again would he look upon that treacherous face of hers. He belonged body and soul to Evelyn, and back to Evelyn he was going. Already he had wasted three weeks. Now it must be another three weeks before he could get to her. Poor darling! What she must be suffering. How heartless she must think him to have sent that rotten cable, invented by Vicky, turning her down; refusing to go to her. He, who knew so well her sensitive, loving nature, could picture how it must have disappointed and upset her. A damnable thing for Vicky to have done; but no more damnable than the other things she had done—to Evelyn—to himself.

Three more weeks before he could get back to Eve—even if he caught a boat to-night—to-morrow —straight back to Cape Town.

He was white under his bronze, and his blue eyes were like hard stones when he finished his packing. Vicky, who had been watching him, shaking from head to foot—made a final appeal. She caught his arm between her long white fingers with their glistening nails—cruel, rapacious fingers.

'Shane—you can't mean to leave me in England —desert me.'

'I do mean to,' he said bluntly. 'And you deserve what you get.'

'But I—I'm your wife.'

'I shall do my level best to get a divorce—and forget I ever married you.'

'I shall never give you a divorce—even if you do desert me for that woman!' she said wildly.

'As you wish,' he said between his teeth. 'Veriland may say likewise—I don't doubt he will. Both of you are rotten enough to do anything disgusting—but it won't make any difference to me—or to Eve, if I know her. We shall go away together—divorced or not.'

'You're cruel—brutal!' said Vicky, and burst into wild weeping.

He looked upon her unmoved.

'Not one quarter so cruel, so brutal, as you and Veriland have been. For months Evelyn has been a martyr to that swine—in order to save her father from prison. And you've helped to hurt her—and me—whom you pretended to care for.'

'It wasn't pretence—I do care.'

'If that's the case, in truth you will suffer as you deserve,' said Shane. And he thought, savagely: 'I'm being spiteful—malicious; but, my God, I feel it—after being tricked and forced into marriage with this woman—and kept away from my darling through her vile treachery.'

Vicky looked at him with stormy eyes, the tears racing down her face.

'You can't get away from the fact that we're married—that once you loved me—held me in your arms.'

That jarred on him. Livid, he answered her:

'You mean that once I *desired* you—basely—as a base woman deserves to be wanted. You mean that once I was intoxicated enough to touch you. Yes, don't I regret it! You needn't remind of *that* night. I shall remember it with disgust—with shame—till I die.'

Vicky cowed back. She began to moan hysterically.

'Oh—oh—I wish I were dead. How cruel you are to me!'

'I daresay my poor Eve has wished herself dead a good many times, living with Veriland,' said Shane, marching to the door. 'Now it's your turn to suffer.'

She snatched at his hand as he passed her.

'Shane—Shane—give me another chance.'

'No,' he said, flinging away her hand. 'It's Eve's turn now—she's never had a chance. You brought this on yourself, remember. Good-bye.'

She screamed after him.

'I've no money—you can't leave your wife to starve— *Shane!*'

He called back to her.

'I'll place an allowance to your credit with your bankers. You can have the damned money. Good-bye.'

That was all. Then he was gone. The big liner was slowing down. Vicky, left alone, knew that they were landing in a few moments.

This was the end of her 'honeymoon,' the finale

to her hopes of happiness. She knew, as she stood there—shivering—sick at heart—badly frightened —that she had played a losing game. She knew, too, that Shane had spoken the truth when he had said she had brought it on herself. For she *had* behaved vilely; that was undeniable.

Yes, she knew she would hurt Evelyn Veriland again if she had a chance. How she *loathed* that woman whom Shane loved.

Would she never see him again?

Yes, she would. She must. She wasn't going to stay behind in England—deserted—humiliated— alone. She would follow her husband back to South Africa on the next boat. She had one big pull—that fact that she had lived with him as his wife. She'd see that neither he nor Evelyn forgot that fact. Besides, if luck was with her, who knew but what that one night of madness on Shane's part would bear fruit—a very lasting and binding reminder of his partnership with her?

She doubled her fists and shook the magnificent red hair back from her tear-filled, glittering eyes. Vicky wasn't beaten yet.

She rang for the stewardess to help her pack her clothes.

XXI

After one shattering, painful scene with her husband at the Queen's Hotel, in Cape Town, Evelyn ran away. She went back to Johannesburg, where she was known to one or two of the well-to-do residents. She was determined to get a job—earn her own living—anything rather than live with Veriland or be beholden to him for her bread and butter again.

'You're penniless and you'll starve if you don't accept my help,' Veriland had shouted at her, in a towering rage when she had announced her intention of leaving him.

'I'd far rather starve and die of starvation than take a penny from you,' she had retorted.

'You're my wife and I'm not going to give you up,' he had told her. 'I shall follow you—make you come back to me.'

'You can't make me come back, and I won't,' she had answered passionately. 'You've ruined my life—separated me from the man I care for—behaved in an abominable, outrageous fashion—I shall never forgive you. I hate you. I've hated you for a long time—and now, thank God, as poor Daddy is out of your reach—there's nothing to prevent me from leaving you.'

'But your wonderful lover is tied up to his cousin and *he* won't come back,' Veriland had sneered as a parting shot.

That was what hurt Evelyn most, now—the only thing, in fact, which had power to hurt her, for she was almost numbed by so much suffering. That cable from Shane had been a blow she had never expected, and it had crushed her. All the joy of life, of living, was gone. All the sunshine had been blotted out of her existence. Life had meant Shane. His love for her—their mutual passion—had been the great burning flame—the inspiration—the breath of life itself. Without it she was defeated and broken. And she was but human—human enough to be madly, bitterly jealous of Vicky. Vicky, who was Shane's wife and whom he meant to stick to now. Yet he had sworn that his marriage meant nothing; that he would never cease to love and want her, Eve.

Had he forgotten so soon? Had Vicky, with her wonderful figure and flaming hair and seductive ways, thawed the ice round his heart—got through his dislike of her and made him her lover?

Unbearable thought! Yet she must bear it. Unceasing agony without Shane; yet that agony must be tolerated. He would never come back. He had said so.

She wanted to die. But death was too great a kindness. She must live on—exist—alone—loving and wanting Shane all her life long.

Tragic and hopeless, Evelyn fled to Johannesburg. But her acquaintances there were of little help. There had been rather too much scandal attached to Mrs. Gordon Veriland and the handsome Shane Cargill of late. Residents had reputations to be preserved. Nobody cared to offer the beautiful Mrs. Veriland a job. Where was Veriland, anyhow? He ought to support her, and she was a little fool if she had run away from him.

Not a hand was lifted in support, in defence of Evelyn. Nobody knew the full facts; nobody could know them; so nobody pitied Evelyn. One or two men who knew her would like to have helped her. She was so young, so very lovely, so charming. But while Veriland was about it was a bit awkward. It seemed wiser to keep out of it.

Evelyn was absolutely alone—stranded with a few pounds in her pockets.

She sold all her expensive dresses—she did not get a tenth of their value. She sold one or two rings which had belonged to her mother. She had left every jewel that Gordon had given her with him at the Queen's in Cape Town. She would not be in his debt for a farthing. It was bad enough to know that her unhappy father had died in debt to

Gordon Veriland.

Poor Daddy! If he but knew what terrible unhappiness he had caused. Evelyn thanked God more than once that he was dead and at peace—out of Veriland's reach.

She found a bed-sitting-room in a quiet, cheap part of the city. It was clean—that was all that could be said of it. Otherwise it was dreadful; so hot that Evelyn could barely stand it.

She was not very strong as yet after her recent nervous breakdown. She was used to a life of luxury, as the wife of a man who was almost a millionaire. The hardships she endured now, struggling along on a few pounds, were real ones—draining her vitality—her courage. It was so difficult to be brave when there was nothing to look forward to in the future.

But there were sweet, wild, beautiful memories to look back upon. And those saved Evelyn in the black weeks of privation; memories and dreams—all of Shane. She felt a grain of comfort in the knowledge that he would never love Vicky as he had loved *her*! No—never. She was sure of that.

She would give half her life to have him back again. Ah, the torment of knowing that had it not been for his marriage to Vicky they might have been together now with nothing to keep them apart. The bitter irony of it. The heartbreak.

Evelyn's eyes were dim with weeping, and she grew so slight, so frail, she was like a flower, wilting in the heat of the city—and so white that she looked like a lily—no colour save in the imperishable gold of her hair.

Gordon Veriland found out where she was living. He pestered her daily. She raged at him, pleaded with him, in turn. Rage and pleading changed to tired indifference. He would not stay away. She grew used to the sight of his big car rolling up every morning; of his hatefully familiar figure stepping out of it, forcing his way into her bed-sitting room. He brought her flowers, fruit, delicacies of every kind. He did his utmost to cajole her into returning to him. As soon as he was gone she gave what he had brought to her landlady, who accepted the expensive gifts, thinking her boarder was slightly mad.

'What's the use of wandering round Johannesburg hunting for work you'll never get?' Gordon asked her one morning when he called in his insistent fashion. 'You're a little fool, Evelyn. Here you are—married to me—one of the richest men in South Africa. Come back and stop thinking about Cargill.'

'I shall never go back to you,' she said.

He scowled at her.

'Damn it—you're worn to a shadow—you'll only get ill and find yourself in a hospital.'

'That would be preferable to any house of yours,' she said, her great grey eyes full of loathing for him.

Veriland, crimson, furious, snarled at her:

'You're crazy. I'll never rest until you do come back to me.'

'Please go and leave me alone,' she said wearily.

He went. But she knew he would come back. How tired she was! Terribly tired of the long, futile struggle and of the pain that nagged all day, all night, in her heart for Shane.

Many weeks had passed since she had rushed madly to Cape Town to try to overtake her lover, and had failed. Six weeks, it must be. Doubtless he had been in London for three weeks now, and was learning to forget her.

How could she know that a cable had been forwarded to her, care of Gordon Veriland, from the Queen's at Cape Town to Veriland's club in Johannesburg? A cable from Shane, telling her that he had only just discovered the truth and was rushing back to her post-haste. But Veriland had torn the message in pieces and did not mean to let his young wife see it. As for Cargill—when he came back to South Africa—well, a lot might happen between now and then.

Veriland continued to persecute his wife and to rely on her failing health in order to get her back. When she fell ill, he would insist that she was taken to a nursing home—not to the general hospital. Money was a great power. Evelyn had none. Therefore he would win in the end, he was confident.

Then Evelyn got a job.

Not a very well-paid one. But a job—which was what she most wanted—to enable her to keep body and soul together. She was to dance as an instructress in a big *palais-de-danse* known as The Summer Garden—then all the rage in Johannesburg. She had answered an advertisement in the local paper for a dance instructress, and her extraordinary grace and beauty had got her the job before one or two other girls who were more experienced in the work and less beautiful.

The hours were long—all the afternoon and evening until midnight. In the heat she found it very trying—especially trying when she had to dance with men who annoyed her or tried to be familiar. And, of course, Gordon followed—came frequently to The Summer Garden and moodily watched his lovely young wife dancing. Her thin face and great tragic eyes were a constant reproach to his brutality.

Then Shane Cargill landed in South Africa; went straight to the Queen's at Cape Town; was told that Gordon Veriland had returned to Johannesburg, and rushed there, hoping against hope to find Evelyn—or at least to trace her.

He would, probably, have gone straight to Veriland's club and demanded Evelyn's address, only he discovered her whereabouts suddenly and unexpectedly almost as soon as he reached the 'gay city' of Rhodesia.

He took a room at one of the big hotels and, dropping into the bar for a cocktail, met an old friend. The friend at once informed him that Evelyn was dancing daily at The Summer Garden.

'Quite a scandal in the city, old man. The wife of a fellow like Veriland who's rolling in money—and she's a paid instructress at The Summer Garden. Thought you'd like to know—used to be a friend of Mrs. Veriland's, didn't you?'

Shane had no answer for this. He left his cocktail untasted. He rushed from the side of his astonished friend and took the first hired car he saw to The Summer Garden, which was in the west end of the city.

Evelyn—dancing as a paid instructress. Then she was not living with Veriland! Thank God for that! Shane's emotions ran riot. He had had three of the longest weeks of his life on board a ship coming over from England. Three weeks of tearing anxiety about Evelyn; of impatience; of regrets.

When he entered the big dance-hall he saw the woman he loved—saw her at once. He would have picked her out from a thousand others. There she was—slim, too slim, exquisitely graceful. Infinitely weary was the look on her lovely face as she danced round the room with a big Colonial in whom she had no interest and who seemed to Shane's jealous eye to be very interested in her.

Shane—always impulsive—marched straight across that shining dance-floor and cut in between the two.

'My dance, I think,' he said.

'Say——' began the Colonial.

'Shane. *Shane!*' said Evelyn in such a heart-rending voice that the Colonial surprised and abashed, retired.

Evelyn's heart seemed to stop beating. Shane stood there before her, his arms around her, oblivious of every other person in the room. Shane, looking thin and haggard and bronzed after his sea-voyage. But Shane just as she remembered him—amazingly youthful and good-looking, with those blazing blue eyes under their thick black lashes and his sudden, flashing, magnetic smile. She felt her knees tremble under her. The sight and sound of him after six or seven weeks of such hell as she had passed through completely unnerved her.

'Oh, it can't be you!' she whispered.

'Hold up, Sweetheart,' he said, and guided her off the dance-floor to a remote corner and put her gently in a chair. She had turned so white that it frightened him. But the colour came speeding back to her cheeks and the light to her eyes. She held out both hands dumbly. He kissed them.

'I don't care a damn who sees. Oh, Eve. *Eve!*'

'Shane, Sweetheart,' she gasped. 'Where have you come from? I thought you were in London.'

'I was in Southampton for one hour only,' he said tensely, keeping her hands locked in his. 'Then I came back on a boat which was just sailing—got a berth by the luck of the devil.'

'But—where is Vicky?'

'I don't know and don't care.'

'Shane—what's happened?'

He told her, briefly, tersely. Enlightenment came to her. She knew that he had never written that cool cable which had shattered her hopes and broken her heart all over again. She knew that they were both victims of further treachery on Vicky's part.

'Did you get my cable, telling you I was coming back?' he asked her.

'No, never,' she said. 'Gordon must have seen to that.'

Shane's lips were a hard line.

'He won't see to anything more of the sort—neither will that unfortunate woman I married. Eve, you and I are going away together—right now.'

She could not speak. She looked at him speechlessly, her very soul in her eyes. To have him back; to know that he loved her as much—nay more—than ever, and that all was going to be well between them, was an ecstasy beyond words.

Then she said, brokenly:

'Gordon will never divorce me.'

'Vicky says she won't divorce me—but do we care? We ought to; but are we going to let it separate us—after all we've suffered?' he asked passionately.

'No, no, we can't part again,' she whispered.

'Oh, my Sweet—we can't—we won't,' he said.

He made her break her contract at The Summer Garden. He told the manager he would pay the necessary sum of money in lieu of notice. He drove Evelyn in a car back to her lodgings.

'To-morrow we will leave this infernal town—this infernal country—go to the ends of the earth together,' he said.

She was in his arms, hat off, pale gold head crushed against his shoulder, lips burning under the passion of his kisses. An aching sweetness and languor enveloped her. The long agony of months seemed assuaged in the warmth and strength of his embrace.

'Shane, Shane—my darling—I've never for an instant forgotten you,' she said. 'Darling, please tell me you never forgot me, either.'

'Never for an instant!' he said. Then looked over the pale gold head that he adored, and suddenly shame burnt a deep red in the tan of his skin. That wasn't true. He *had* forgotten—that first night out at sea—drugged by drink—by a woman's physical allure. How he loathed the remembrance of Vicky! But that must be forgotten and blotted out, and why hurt Evelyn by telling her?

The arranged to meet at her lodgings on the following day. To-night he would come and take her out to dinner. They could not bear to be apart for a single hour.

They went back to his hotel like one treading on air. The idea that to-morrow he could take this idolised woman away and never leave her again was an intoxication in itself.

He walked into his bedroom, whistling like a boy. But he stopped short in the doorway and the happiness was wiped from his face as though by a sponge.

A woman stood by the windows—a tall, voluptuous figure in pale grey chiffon with a big grey hat on her red head.

Vicky had followed him.

Relentlessly he looked at her.

'So you've come after me, have you? Well, it isn't any good, and you'd better spare both of us a painful scene and go away again,' he said harshly.

Vicky's lashes hid what lay in her eyes. Her hands plucked nervously at the lizard bag she carried. She said, in a very nervous voice:

'Shane—one moment. I—I know I—you meant not to see me again—but I—had to come.'

'Why?'

'I followed you out at first because I was in a panic—about losing you. But later—for another reason.'

'There can only be one reason—to irritate me,' said Shane. 'For heaven's sake go away and put an end to all this business. I've seen Evelyn and she and I are clearing out of South Africa together tomorrow morning.'

Vicky came close to him.

'Are you?' she said in a low voice. 'Do you think it a fair or decent thing to run away with this girl from the woman who is bearing—your child?' The sudden bolt went home. Shane Cargill stared—went from white to red and red to white again—then felt a queer, sick, frightened sensation in his heart.

Vicky gave a queer smile. She was using a weapon which she knew would be very effective. She added:

'I am going to have a baby, Shane. The result of that—one night—on board. Do you remember?'

Did he remember? Oh, God, yes, to his undying shame and regret. But surely it had not borne such fruit—surely fate and circumstance would not deal him this monstrous blow?

He staggered and caught at the back of a chair to

steady himself.

'I don't believe it—it's a trick—another of your treacherous lies!' he stammered.

'It's true,' she said. 'You can see my doctor. He will tell you—he told me, definitely last night.'

That finished Shane. He dropped into a chair—stared up at her for a moment—saw that her face was thinner, her eyes tired, her vivid good looks dimmed by ill-health. And he supposed that she was—at last—speaking the truth.

She dropped on her knees beside him and seized his hands.

'Shane, Shane, whatever I've done, you can't go away with Evelyn and desert me—now—when I'm expecting your child.'

He did not push her away. He was too stunned. It was a monstrous blow—a frightful lesson indeed. Why hadn't he kept his head that night? Why had he drunk himself into a state of recklessness? What would Evelyn think and say now that this thing had happened?

'Shane,' came Vicky's husky voice, 'you like children, don't you? You wouldn't care to think of me bearing a child to you—alone—unprotected. After all—you *are* my husband and the child's father. You ought to stand by me now.'

Then he sprang up—blazing-eyed—furious—almost demented.

'It isn't fair—it's hideously unjust—when Evelyn and I love each other. I won't be coerced into staying with you. I don't care whether you're going to have a child or not. I won't desert Evelyn now, at the eleventh hour, after all she's gone through.'

Vicky stood up, wiping her lips with a handkerchief. She was trembling.

'Very well, Shane, if you won't do the decent thing.'

'Decent!' he broke in, and laughed discordantly. 'Heavens above—do you know the meaning of the word *decency*, when this—this thing you've done is the most cowardly, mean, *indecent* thing of all?'

She cowed a little, and began to laugh and cry together.

'So you mean to quit me—and go away with Evelyn?'

'Yes.' Shane put both clenched hands to his head. 'Yes.'

'All right. We'll see what she says about it.'

Vicky moved to the door. Shane sprang after her.

'What devil's work are you going to do now?'

She faced him defiantly.

'I'm going to Mrs. Veriland. I shall tell her—everything. Perhaps she doesn't know about that night on board. Anyhow, even if she forgave it, she won't be a party to you deserting the mother of your child. No true woman would. You say she's so sweet and gentle and kind. Well, we'll see if she'll take my child's father away.'

She laughed hysterically and ran out of the room. Shane stared after her, dumbfounded.

XXII

When Shane fully realised what Vicky meant to do, he was like a madman. He tore out of the room after her. She had disappeared. The page at the door in the vestibule told him that a red-haired lady in grey had just taken a hired car away from the hotel.

So she had gone to Evelyn! Through his own unhappy folly all their happiness would be destroyed and the city of their dreams laid in ruins about them!

Shane, white and grim, went back to his room and, sitting down, put his handsome head between his hands. He thought hard, feverishly, desperately. He sat there for fully a quarter of an hour without moving, asking himself what he had better do now. Then he jumped to his feet. He must go round to Evelyn's rooms at once and make sure whether Vicky was really going to do this damnable thing.

He sat in a car, driving through Johannesburg, which had grown suddenly dark, at the ending of the perfect day, and he prayed, as he had not prayed since he was a small boy, that this catastrophe would not happen to him and the woman he loved.

Evelyn was putting the last touch to a very charming toilet when Vicky arrived at her rooms. She was sitting in front of her dressing-table polishing her pretty filbert nails. She was dressed in a long white chiffon dress; imitation pinky pearls about her slender throat; a spray of pink carnations on her shoulder. She had chosen to wear white—like a bride—for Shane who had come back as from the dead. She had bought the flowers, recklessly—forgetting she had had to pinch and scrape and economise lately. She wanted to look lovely—for him. And her cheeks were as deep pink as the carnations, her grey eyes like stars.

'Shane, Shane!' She repeated his name softly as she passed the polisher over her nails. And now and then remembering the hot passion of his lips. his possessive hands, his handsome, ardent eyes, a wild thrill of ecstasy shot through her.

She had loved this man for a long time better than any human being on earth. She had lost him for a little while; and now he had come back and this time nothing on earth would separate them. Her father was dead. There was nothing to keep them apart. Neither felt they owed duty to the people they had married—whom they had been unjustly *forced* to marry.

Then Vicky came into the room. Evelyn's landlady showed her in and announced her without ceremony:

'Mrs. Shane Cargill wants to see you, Miss Mayton.'

Evelyn had been using her maiden name, dancing in Johannesburg.

Evelyn sprang up. The nail-polisher dropped from her fingers. The radiance was wiped from her face. She stared at Shane's wife in a startled fashion. *Mrs. Cargill!* How that name jarred on every nerve.

Vicky, looking rather pale, but with her head held defiantly high, looked at Evelyn with sullen eyes.

'I want to speak to you,' she said.

And she told herself, writhing, that Evelyn looked a perfect picture—much too lovely. No wonder Shane had always been crazy about this woman. A man well might sell his soul for that exquisite figure, the pale gold lustre of the hair framing an angelic young face—a face that was an enchanting mixture of passion and purity. Vicky hated her. Hated her for the hold she had over Shane. She added:

'I've something very important to say.'

Evelyn, quite calm and very grave, said:

'You can have nothing to say to me—surely.'

'Oh, no?' said Vicky in a sneering voice. 'That's queer, considering you and *my* husband were on the eve of running away together.'

Evelyn's colour deepened, but she remained calm. She had been hurt badly by this girl's treachery, and she saw no reason why she should not do the thing she and Shane had agreed to do. She said, quietly:

'It is quite true, Shane and I *are* going away to-morrow.'

'I wonder you aren't ashamed——' began Vicky.

'One moment,' broke in Evelyn with calm dignity. 'Don't run away with the idea that I am stealing your husband. Such is not the case. Shane and I have cared for each other for a long time. My husband, whom you know had an unfair power over me through my father, kept me from Shane. Then you came along and betrayed us and widened the gulf between us—what's more, you blackmailed Shane into marriage with you. Why should I, under these circumstances, be ashamed to go away with Shane to-morrow, now that my father is dead?'

Vicky sat down and crossed her legs and, taking a cigarette from her bag, coolly lit it.

'You can't go off with Shane to-morrow,' she said. 'No matter how you feel about the right or wrong of it.'

Evelyn bit her lip. She began to feel irritated by the presence of this girl.

'Please,' she said, 'let's understand each other.'

'We will, when I've said what I want to say.'

'And what is that?'

'Only this. You can't take my husband away from me, because if you do it will be a sin and shame on your part. I'm going to have a child. *Shane's child!* Now what about it?'

Dead silence. Evelyn stared. The beautiful carnation-pink faded from her face, leaving it as white as her chiffons. He eyes dilated. Then she blushed burning scarlet to the roots of her golden hair.

'That isn't true,' she said in a choked voice. 'It can't possibly be true.'

'And why not?'

'You and Shane—haven't—lived together.' She stumbled over the words.

'Oh, but we have,' said Vicky. 'On board ship going to England.'

Evelyn looked down at her, a deepening horror in her eyes, and a sick sensation in her heart.

'You—you—*mean* that?'

'I can prove it. Besides, Shane will tell you it's true. I've just seen him. He couldn't deny he was my baby's father. He knows he is.'

Then Evelyn felt the room swim round her. She couldn't breathe. She stumbled to the window and stood leaning against the sill, letting the night air blow upon her. She said more to herself than Vicky:

'It can't be true. God, don't let it be true!'

Vicky's voice reached her, whining now:

'You wouldn't be so mean as to run off with Shane now, would you, Evelyn? I know I behaved rottenly to you both, but I'm sorry for that now—I can't help having the baby, can I? Shane says he's going to take you away anyhow, despite it. But you won't go—you're decent, Evelyn—you wouldn't consider it the right thing—to desert me when I'm like this—and rob my child—*his* child—of a father?'

Evelyn closed her eyes. She shuddered. She wanted to put her hands to her ears and shut out the sound of that whining, cunning voice which slowly but surely was tearing the happiness up by the roots out of her very heart, leaving a bleeding gap. She had been so happy a few minutes ago. She put her hands to her burning eyelids. It was a nightmare, surely—all that this woman was telling her about her wedding night on board and Shane's passionate love-making. She'd wake up in a second to feel Shane's arms about her and hear him answer her that all was well and that never had he forgotten her.

Had he, indeed, been disloyal to their love? Had he taken this red-haired woman to his heart?

Evelyn found a chair, sank into it, hid her face in her hands.

'You won't go with him—steal a poor little baby's father,' continued the whining, tearful voice of Vicky.

'Stop a moment,' broke in Evelyn, agonised. 'Stop—please. I can't believe it—it can't be true.'

'But you won't take him from me—now?'

Evelyn looked at her blindly.

'If you are really the mother of Shane's child—no!' she said hoarsely.

Vicky gave a great sigh of relief.

'Well, I am—and I think it's splendid of you, Evelyn,' she said with triumph in her eyes.

The door opened noisily. Shane Cargill burst into the room—Shane, looking desperate, hunted, white under his tan and with a sick horror in his eyes that she could understand. She stood up and looked at him. He looked back, speechlessly. Vicky sat, sniffing, a handkerchief to her lips.

Evelyn's very soul seemed to die within her. She read the ugly truth in Shane's eyes long before he uttered a word. Read shame in those handsome eyes—and guilt. So it was true. Her world crashed in ruins around her in that instant. She was the first to speak:

'Shane—your—wife tells me she is—expecting—a—child—your child. Is it true?'

'I suppose it is,' he said between his teeth. 'Oh—my God—what a thing to have happened!'

Vicky stood up and looked at him sullenly.

'Well, it *has* happened, and Evelyn says she won't take you off. Your place is with me, under the circumstances.'

Shane did not seem to hear her. His eyes were riveted on Evelyn. The loveliness and grace of her in that long white dress, with the pink pearls about her throat, and the carnations on her shoulder and the sheen of her golden hair. The sweet beauty of her, whom he had always loved so well! He realised that she was ready dressed for their dinner. Their *reunion* dinner, it was to have been. The hideous cruelty of this thing that had happened smote him like a blast and withered him up.

'Eve—let me explain——' he began.

'There can't be any but the most obvious explanation,' she said coldly. The very coldness of her voice made his heart sink like a plummet. Already there was an immense distance between them—an unbridgable gulf—built up by Vicky's spiteful hands. And a few hours ago Evelyn had lain in his arms, yielding, adoring, giving kiss for kiss. It was unbearable.

'Eve——' he cried.

'I don't want you to tell me anything,' she broke in hysterically, 'except the truth. *Have* you lived with this woman as your wife, and *is* she the mother of your child?'

'Yes,' muttered Vicky.

'I—yes!' The confession was wrung from Shane. 'But only once——'

'That's all I want to know.' She was ice-cold now. Her grey eyes blazed bitter reproach and wounded passion. He, who had sworn fidelity, told her he had never for an instant forgotten her, was no longer the Shane of her fervid imagination. He was just a weak, ordinary man who could make love to any woman so long as he was in the mood and she sufficiently attractive. After her long agony of loving and wanting him, her utter constancy, the thing hit her on the raw. 'Good-bye—both of you,' she added.

'Eve—for God's sake.'

'Please take your wife away. There can be no question now of our—going away to-morrow. Your place is with the woman who is bearing your child,' she said, very coldly and proudly.

'She's quite right,' said Vicky, then began to weep. 'Shane, how can you look at me so cruelly— when I'm ill—and tired out?'

It was a terrible moment for the man. A moment when he realised only too well what that night of intoxication on board ship had cost him. Fundamentally he had never been unfaithful to Evelyn, but in that drunken stupor he had betrayed their love. And now he must pay for it—a bitter and heavy price. The loss of Evelyn—the cup of happiness snatched from their lips. What she must feel about it hurt him as much as his own pain.

The sound of Vicky's weeping exasperated him. His nerves were raw—torn to shreds. He tried to remember that she was the mother of his child and that Evelyn was exiling him with Vicky—for always.

'If you won't let me speak,' he said hoarsely, 'then I can't make you understand, Eve. Good-bye.'

He took Vicky's arm and led her out of the room.

Evelyn gave one anguished glance at the door that closed between them, then fell downwards on her bed—arms outstretched—like one crucified with grief. The pearls about her neck snapped—rolled on to the floor. The carnations were crushed, and the room was filled with the sound of passionate, bitter weeping.

In that dark hour—the darkest, perhaps, of her life—Evelyn was not hurt so much by the knowledge that she had lost all chance of happiness with her lover as by the feeling that he had been unfaithful to her and their love. Another woman would bear his son—not she, who had loved him for so long and devotedly.

That broke Evelyn's heart—if it was not already broken.

XXIII

If ever there was a desperate and tortured man in Johannesburg that night, it was Shane Cargill. He was tortured with remorse for his own folly, for the wrong he had done Evelyn. He felt he had wronged Vicky too, although he knew, in his heart, that Vicky had instigated the whole thing—played an unfair game—and won it.

He could not tolerate the idea that he had lost Evelyn. Long after he had put his wife in an hotel and left her, he paced the streets of the city under the stars, grim, seething, racked by maddening emotions.

He was haunted by the memory of Evelyn—so fair, so lovely, so proud—ordering him to take Vicky away and leave her. Perhaps she was right. His place *was* with her the mother of his child. On the other hand, why should he pay all his life for one hour of passion? Why, when he had married Vicky to save Evelyn's father? It wasn't fair of her to cast him into utter darkness for that one moment of weakness. Surely she ought to be more understanding of men, more sympathetic. Vicky had blackmailed him into marrying her. What duty did he owe her—even if she *was* to have a child?

The hours went by. Shane still walked the streets, like a madman crazy with grief and contrition, until his emotions culminated into hot resentment against Evelyn for refusing to hear his explanation.

He had been temporarily down and out; shattered by the blow fate had dealt him. But Shane Cargill was no weakling. He was a passionate, impulsive man—used to defying fate and circumstance. The old spirit of devil-may-care returned.

Damn it all, he wasn't going to be the victim of destiny like this; neither was he going to give up Evelyn without a good struggle.

It was striking eleven o'clock when Shane Cargill, grim about the lips, blue eyes a little crazed, marched into Evelyn's rooms. Her landlady—scandalised—told him that Miss Mayton had gone to The Summer Garden to dance as usual.

Shane sat down to wait. The landlady shrugged her shoulders. These dancers had queer morals, but it was no business of hers, and the gentleman said it was urgent business.

Evelyn came back from The Summer Garden at ten minutes past twelve. Weary, tired, in heart as well as body, drooping like a wilting lily, she came slowly into her bed-sitting-room and found Shane Cargill standing in it, smoking a cigarette. There were a great many ends in the ash-tray on the table.

Her heart gave an agonised jerk.

'Why are you here?'

'I had to see you, Evelyn,' he said tersely. 'Why were you at that dance-place? You agreed to throw it up.'

She laid her cloak on a chair and smoothed back a strand of fair hair with a weary gesture that touched him deeply. Poor darling! she was worn out—her eyes looked enormous and shadowy in her pale young face.

'I was going to chuck the job—when I first saw you again—but circumstances are different now,' she said. 'I asked the manager to take me back. Unfortunately, when we gave notice this evening, he immediately engaged another girl; so I've lost my job.'

'That doesn't matter,' said Shane. He came up to her. 'Evelyn—this can't go on. It's damned silly. You're coming away with me—as we arranged.'

'Oh, no—not now. Your place is with Vicky.'

His temper blazed out. He was in a state of nerves, and control snapped easily. He caught her wrists and swung her into his arms.

'To hell with that. My place is with you, and you know it. Eve, I *won't* be chucked out—I won't be condemned to spend the rest of my life with a woman I despise.'

'Shane—let me go!' she said, gasping, very white. 'Remember—the woman you say you despise—is bearing your child.'

'I do remember it, to my undying regret!' he said between his teeth.

'To your shame,' she broke out with sudden bitter passion. 'You—who swore to be faithful.'

'One moment. You don't understand—you wouldn't let me tell you—but now you must hear and know. This child is the result of one single night of folly. It was the first night on board. I hadn't had your wire about your father, remember. I felt crushed by the thought that I'd lost you. I wanted to forget—I couldn't endure the pain—I got tight—yes, I admit it—I drank—became like a beast. And then that vile woman got me. I woke up in the morning to realise what I'd done—and loathed myself and her. Eve—Eve——' His passionate voice broke, and he caught and held her close, burying his shamed face against her breast. 'You must believe it, darling. I've never loved any woman but you. It was a frightful piece of folly. But don't punish me for it. Eve, I love you so. Let's go away to-morrow—oh, my God, darling, don't turn from me now!'

Evelyn lay quiescent in his arms for a moment. All this evening she had ached for those arms. But her face was contorted, her lips twisted with bitter pain. She tried to understand his weakness—a man's weakness. Men were built like that. They must needs find solace and forgetfulness from their pain in drink or in the arms of another woman. But a woman must suffer without an anodyne—hopelessly, acutely—and remain uncomforted. She loved him so much—she tried to make excuses in her heart. But there was always the child—the fruit of his folly. She could not forget that.

'Forgive me—take me back—go away with me,' he implored her, his handsome face white and racked with feeling.

'No, no, I can't—Shane, let me go!'

'Don't you love me any more, Eve?'

'That isn't the point,' she panted, straining away from him. 'You've got your wife and child to think of.'

'No, no, I refuse to think of them. I love only you. Eve—Sweetheart—you must go with me.'

'No, Shane—not now.'

'Yes, you must.' He forced her back into his embrace, kissed her wildly on the lips, the eyes, the throat. He tried, by the very strength of his passion, to weaken her resolve to part from him. He was demented—and she, loving him with every bit of her, felt as though she were drowning—dying there against his heart. Her lips ached under his— her body yielded—she was terribly tempted. It was so easy to give in; to say: 'Yes, take me—let's forget Vicky.'

But she remembered that once *she* had been about to bear Shane a child. She could not allow Shane to abandon Vicky now. She must conquer her own desires and send him back to his wife.

'Let me go, Shane,' she gasped. 'Go away—I won't listen to you any more. Please, please go!'

He lifted his head and looked at her, his eyes stricken. Passion died, leaving only a great aching pain in his heart.

'Do you really want me to go, Eve?'

'Yes,' she muttered. 'Yes, you must go. Your duty lies with the mother of your child. It's your own fault, Shane.'

'Oh, God—don't remind me of that!' he said, scarlet to the roots of his thick, dark hair.

'I'm sorry,' she stammered. 'But go now, please!'

He gave a last look at her, then stumbled out of the room. He walked back to his hotel in the bright moonlight like an automaton. He thought:

'This is the absolute end.'

The end—the result of his own one crazy folly. Now the devil-may-care feeling had passed. He was a broken-hearted man; broken and defeated. He had left Evelyn broken and vanquished too.

It seemed to Shane Cargill the very end of the world for them both.

XXIV

About a month later, Evelyn sat in the lounge of The Summer Garden, toying with a cup of tea in the company of a fair, slimly built young man who had a pair of bright hazel eyes and a cheerful, rather jolly smile.

The young man was the new manager of The Summer Garden. Four weeks ago Evelyn had applied to him for her old job and he had been unable to give it to her because he had arranged a contract with another girl when she had first broken her contract, believing that she was going to leave South Africa with Shane.

Since then Evelyn and her one-time manager had seen rather a lot of each other. Geoffrey Sparnell was nice—more than ordinarily nice—and good at his job. A gentleman by birth and education, he had come out to Johannesburg and stepped into the job, straight from Oxford. His uncle was owner of The Summer Garden and many other big public institutions in the city.

Sparnell was in love with Evelyn. He had realised right from the start that she was no ordinary instructress. Her enchanting blonde beauty and personal magnetism coupled with that air of tragedy, of sorrow, made her doubly attractive to Geoffrey Sparnell. But being rather an upright young man—knowing that she was married—he had never deliberately pursued her.

A week ago, however, in touch with her, trying to help her find work, she had told him that

Gordon Veriland was dead. And once she was free Geoffrey no longer followed the path of platonic friendship. He told her, at once, that he was passionately in love with her and besought her to marry him.

Evelyn had refused him every day for a week. She did not want to marry him, although she liked him and valued his friendship. He was of her own age and gay and clean and all that a woman might want. But she felt that her heart was dead and buried—with Shane—that so far as passion was concerned, she, Evelyn, had died that night she had sent Shane away from her.

It had come as an extra piece of irony, on the part of fate, to hear that Gordon was dead and that she was a widow. Veriland had been the victim of a motor accident in Cape Town and was killed instantaneously. But financially Evelyn did not benefit by his death. Out of sheer spite he had made a will recently, bequeathing all his money to a distant relative rather than that Evelyn should have it. Not that she would have taken his money in any case.

But here she was—so absolutely free now—and once when Shane had been her lover she would have given much for this freedom. The position filled her with great bitterness.

'You look so thin and pale, Evelyn darling,' Geoffrey Sparnell told her this afternoon, his anxious eyes watching her every gesture. 'I wish to God you'd marry me and let me take you away to the sea.'

'I wish I could care for you that way, Geoff,' she said with a sad smile.

Sparnell scowled.

'Damn this fellow Cargill,' he muttered.

Evelyn closed her eyes wearily. What use to damn Shane? What had happened had happened, and could not be undone. But she wished desperately that the pain in her heart which was for Shane would stop for just a brief while. It went on nagging, nagging, driving her mad. She had neither seen him nor heard from him all this month. But a mutual acquaintance had told her he was still in the city and had been seen driving with a red-haired girl. Vicky, his wife, of course. Oh, but Evelyn was jealous—madly, horribly jealous of Vicky—of her rights—of her hopes. It all hurt, horribly, day and night.

'Can't you ever forget this affair and marry me, Evelyn?' young Sparnell persisted, and leaned across the little table and put a hand over hers.

He did not irritate her, neither was he physically repellent. He was a good-looking, charming boy, and he had a position and money to come. But she could not love him; she could only remember the hard, brown, possessive figure of Shane, her lover. She felt as though she was dying—by inches—wanting him.

'Evelyn, give me some hope,' said Geoffrey Sparnell huskily.

She looked at him with her sad grey eyes—eyes the colour of rain-washed wood-violets, he thought, with passionate pity for her in his heart.

She thought, wearily:

'Why not accept him? I've got no job, no friends, no prospects, no hope of anything but loneliness and pain. Shane is with Vicky—will have his child later. Am I not a fool not to take Geoffrey's love?'

On a crazy impulse—wounded to death—desperately lonely, Evelyn said:

'If I do marry you, Geoff—will it be fair? I can't

love you—that way.'

'I'll risk it,' he said eagerly. His sunburnt face grew warm and eager. 'I'll make you love me—when you're my wife.'

'No,' she said. 'No man will ever stir me to a single thrill.'

'I can and will,' he said with passion. 'I don't believe this other chap has killed everything in you.'

'Not only he, Geoff. Life—pain—the whole wretched disaster of it all.'

'Marry me,' he repeated. 'Let me take care of you.'

'Very well—if you'll take me, knowing I don't care,' she said wearily. 'But it's hard on you.'

'Evelyn—it means heaven to me!' he said, and his eyes glowed. He pressed her hand ardently under the table. 'Sweetheart—do you mean it?'

She nodded her golden head. But her heart ached, and she thought:

'*He* used to call me Sweetheart. Oh, Shane—*Shane!*'

She was in the mood when she did not much care what she did, what happened. Geoffrey Sparnell soared to the stars, madly in love, madly happy because she had accepted him. He was so certain he would win her love in the end.

Then; toward the end of that month, Shane Cargill heard that young Sparnell of The Summer Garden was going to be married the next day. Casually he asked the name of the bride. When he was told that it was Evelyn Veriland he nearly went mad.

All these weeks he had kept away from Evelyn, tried hard to be dutiful to Vicky, to show her kindness, if nothing else, because of her condition, and to resign himself to separation from the woman he loved. But he had never for an instant felt resignation. He grew more bitter, more resentful, with every day that passed. Vicky was fretful and difficult, and frayed his nerves until he felt he could not stay with her and remain sane. And it hit him hard, just as it had hit Evelyn, to hear of Veriland's death and realise that Evelyn was free.

This was the last straw—this news that Evelyn was going to marry Geoffrey Sparnell. For an hour after Shane heard about it he brooded over the matter; pictured Evelyn in Geoffrey Sparnell's arms; pictured her giving him all the grace, the beauty, the sweetness that had been his, Shane's, and was intrinsically his for ever.

He took out his big racing car and drove in it like a madman to Evelyn's rooms.

He had made up his mind, definitely, that no other man on earth should marry Evelyn and possess her. She belonged to him. Vicky and the child could be provided for. But he was going to take Evelyn away. *He was going to take her by force if she wouldn't go of her own free will.*

XXV

Evelyn, on the eve of her wedding, was far from being a normal, happy bride-to-be. As every hour brought her nearer to the fate that she had voluntarily accepted, she grew very quiet—so quiet, indeed, that Geoffrey Sparnell was worried and a little vexed. He was madly in love with her, and it very naturally irked him to see her looking paler than usual, with a stunned sort of expression in those great, lovely eyes and a set look about her sweet lips, as though she was making a great effort.

It was true, of course, that she was making an

effort to appear as her fiancé wished her to be—acquiescent, content. And of these two things she was only capable of the first. She could and did acquiesce when he took her in his arms, and did allow him to kiss, to caress her. But passively, like a slim, pale statue in his embrace. There was no ardour in her blood for Geoffrey Sparnell, and bitter resentment against the whole scheme of things raged fiercely where love's contentment should have reigned. She was making herself marry Geoffrey because she believed it the best thing to do. He wanted her at any price. She felt that he would be good to her, and she was 'up against it.' She would be a fool to turn him down. It was best, too, for Shane—for Vicky. Now that Shane was so utterly separated from her by the fruits of his own unhappy folly, it was so futile to stay alone and grieve over the past. It would, perhaps, help him, she thought, when he knew that she was more or less happily married and beyond his reach.

But even Evelyn did not quite know her lover. It was impossible for Shane to regard Evelyn as beyond his reach. And impossible for him to sit quiet under the blow of the knowledge that she was on the eve of giving herself for ever to Geoffrey Sparnell.

When Geoffrey took her back to her rooms that evening—she had spent an afternoon with him, shopping—Evelyn was amazed and perturbed to find Shane waiting for her. Shane like a raging tiger, pacing up and down her sitting-room with a white, set face, burning eyes, and evidences of his unrest in a few dozens of cigarette-ends on the ashtray on the table by the window.

Evelyn looked at him with dread in her soul. Yes, she dreaded seeing him. One glimpse of that loved, attractive face—that man so fatally attractive to her—and every drop of blood in her body was coursing crazily through her veins. She still loved him so terribly. What use the resignation—the endeavour, all to-day, to be sweet and tender to Geoffrey? Geoffrey ceased to exist for her now that Shane stood before her.

But Geoffrey was very much there, at her side, to-day, and when he entered the room, bearing her parcels for her, his good-looking young face was as pale as Shane's and almost as fierce. He knew at once who this was. Cargill—Cargill, whom he loathed, although he had never spoken two words to him, but whom he knew was Evelyn's former lover. He disliked him with all a boy's crazy jealousy. And underlying the jealousy ran the swift, impulsive thought:

'What a handsome swine he is—*damn him*!'

It was impossible for anybody to look at Shane's great, muscular, beautifully built body—at that leonine head with its dark, thick hair; the brown, fine face with the sculptured features; the stronger jaw, the passionate lips—and not admit his magnificence.

The two men glared at each other. Strangers, yet deadly rivals. Evelyn, very composed outwardly, although she was inwardly a tornado, advanced toward Shane and said, quietly:

'Why have you come?'

'Because I had to,' he said. His voice was hoarse. She could see, now that she was close to him, how the strain had told on him. He looked years older. A desperate pity surged in her heart for him. Oh, her darling, her life—her one love—if only she could draw that haggard, twitching face down to her breast and cradle it there and comfort him!

But he belonged to Vicky and to his coming child. With a great effort she said:

'You ought not to have come. You know—I am to be married to-morrow. This is—Mr. Sparnell—whom I am marrying.'

Shane bit hard at his lip. He looked at Geoffrey. Geoffrey put Evelyn's parcels on the table and scowled back. Shane said between his teeth:

'You will never marry him, Eve.'

Then the younger man's temper flared. He came forward, hands clenched at his sides.

'Look here—there are limits. What the hell——'

'Oh—wait—please!' broke in Evelyn. She trembled, sick and sorry that these two had met. Why had Shane come? Why make her suffer unnecessarily?

'Shane—*please*!' she protested.

'Evelyn, I was told you were to be married to-morrow. You can't—you can't do it!' he said.

She blinded herself to the agony in those blue, haunted eyes of his.

'Shane, I am going to do it. You must go away and let me alone—leave me in peace. This isn't fair.'

'Fair!' he echoed bitterly. 'Oh, for God's sake, is anything in life fair? Was it fair that you married Veriland instead of me—or that I married Vicky—or any of the damnable things that have happened to you and me?'

'Look here——' began young Sparnell again. He was revolted by the whole conversation and jealous to the core of his being, because he had seen a look flame into Evelyn's eyes, when she saw this Cargill, that had never flamed for *him*.

'No, Geoff—let me speak, please,' Evelyn begged him.

'What's the use of it?' he said sullenly.

'Evelyn belongs to me,' said Shane.

'To the devil with that,' said Sparnell hotly. 'You're married. Good God, man——'

'Oh, be quiet!' broke in Evelyn, exasperated, her nerves in shreds. 'Let me end this. Leave it to me, Geoff. Now, Shane, I beg you to go. You make everything so difficult—and it's no use. Please go!'

He stared down at the white, set young face. He said huskily:

'Eve, how can you marry this man when you still love me?'

'We've had it all out,' she said wearily. 'You belong to the mother of your child.'

'Is that the only reason you're booting me? Because of the child?'

'Yes. You know it.'

'Oh, *God*!' he said, and put a hand to his eyes.

Geoffrey Sparnell looked away from him. He hated and despised the fellow, but he did not like to see such anguish on the face of any human being. He knew the whole story. Evelyn had told him. He loved Evelyn, so he could guess what this fellow, Cargill, was suffering. But he wanted Evelyn himself, and to-morrow was their wedding-day. He was damned if he would give her up now. He was in a fever of anxiety for Cargill to go.

'Evelyn,' he broke out. 'You've promised——'

'All right, Geoff,' she said tersely. 'I won't break my word. Be patient.'

Relieved, he turned away, lit a cigarette, and wondered, gloomily, if he would ever be able to fight the memory of Cargill in Evelyn's mind, even if he married her and separted her, physically, from him.

Shane, as though Sparnell did not exist, came

nearer Evelyn and took both her hands.

'Dearest—dearest!' he said in a passionate undertone. 'You can't marry any man on earth but me.'

'Oh, Shane, don't. I can't marry you—you know it,' she said, and caught her breath on a sob. She tried to drag her fingers from his. 'Don't—please. You're hurting me so.'

'Eve—I, too, am hurt to the death,' he said. 'I can't tolerate the idea of you married. Come away with me. Forget everything.'

'No,' she broke in. 'I'm marrying Geoff to-morrow.'

'You mean that?' he said incredulously.

'I mean it.'

Sparnell, gnawing at his finger-nail, heard and rejoiced. Thank God! She wasn't going back on him. She was wonderful—loyal. He adored her.

But Shane Cargill dropped Evelyn's hands and looked as though she had put a knife straight through him.

'You've got to choose between us—for good and all. And you choose—Geoffrey Sparnell?'

'Yes,' she said, very white, very determined, and with a heart-broken look in her eyes.

Then Shane turned on his heel and walked blindly out of the room. Evelyn heard the front-door slam. She heard the mighty throb and hum of the big racing car which was so familiar. She stood like a figure carven of stone—listening to the sound of the car die away.

She had banished him finally because it seemed to her the best, the only thing to do. She had shown him definitely that she meant to marry Geoffrey. Once she was married, he would settle down to the idea, and it would be easier for him to do his duty to Vicky and his child.

She was well aware that he had gone away in torment. Oh, wasn't that same torment in her heart for him, and wouldn't it be there for ever?

She suddenly broke into weeping, covering her face with her hands.

She felt Geoffrey's arms go round her.

'Oh, Eve—my darling—Eve.' He caressed her with desperate tenderness, broken-hearted because she cried so terribly and because he adored her.

'Grey-Eyes, don't cry like that.'

Grey-Eyes! His pet-name for her! Poor old Geoff! He loved her. She was moved to pity for him. But pity could not breed passion. She had nothing to give him. She lay against him, mute, limp, her face bathed in bitter tears.

'I loved him, Geoff.'

'I know, but try and love me now. Forget him, my darling. To-morrow you are to be my wife.'

'Yes, I know,' she whispered.

'Do you regret it so terribly? Do you want to back out? Eve, I'm at the end of the tether myself. Don't send me mad.'

'Poor Geoff! Poor boy! I won't go back on you. You heard me tell Shane I was marrying you to-morrow.'

'Does it mean nothing to you?' Sparnell asked in bitterness and with a fever of longing to make her care for him.

'A lot—of course. I value your love. I need your tenderness—your companionship. But don't ask me to love you—as you love me. I can't, Geoff. It isn't in me.'

'He's killed you—the real you,' said Sparnell. 'How I loathe him!'

'Don't. He's very unhappy, Geoff.'

'He shan't have you. You belong to me from to-morrow onwards,' said the boy fiercely, and covered her golden head with kisses.

Exhausted, she begged him to go.

'Leave me now. Let me get some rest—some sleep. Yes, yes, I promise I'll be there, at the registry office, as arranged. No—I swear I won't let you down, Geoff.'

He covered her hands with kisses.

'I'll make you care for me—blot out the memory of that fellow.'

He left her, once again confident that he would win her in the end. But after he had gone, Evelyn lay across her bed, moaning.

'Shane—Shane!'

Blot out the memory of him—that incomparable lover—and their matchless love? No! That wasn't possible. Only death could ease the perpetual ache in her heart, in her soul, for him. Her marriage to-morrow to the boy who wanted her so could not alter her love for Shane. Nothing could. It could only put up another barrier.

She could not forget the awful misery in his eyes when she had told him that she had chosen Geoffrey and sent him from her.

She would have given everything on earth to have him with her now—to feel his arms about her—to hear his voice. If only he had not come. All the wild aching, the blazing fever of the old passion, was destroying her utterly, to-night, until she felt she must wither and die of it.

When she grew calmer, she walked to the window, flung it open wide, and let the cool night air blow upon her fevered cheeks.

The sky blazed with stars. A gorgeous South

African night. She shut her aching eyes and whispered:

'Shane—my darling!'

Suddenly she was gripped by an immense longing to get away out under those stars—to be alone; to visit some spot where she and Shane had been lovers together; to recapture some of the beauty and passion.

To-morrow she would belong to Geoffrey Sparnell. She would go through with the marriage—make him happy if she could not find happiness herself. To-night she still belonged to Shane.

Geoffrey had given her a small car for a wedding present. She would go out—drive—somewhere—anywhere—and forget to-morrow for a little while.

Hatless, with just a tweed coat over the thin, flowered *crêpe de Chine* dress which she was wearing, Evelyn steered her small car out of the garage.

At seven o'clock she was driving swiftly up the mountains. She knew where she wanted to go. She was mastered by the impulse to revisit Shane's shooting-box—that dear little pine-log cabin to which he had taken her months ago. It seemed, now, a thousand years back.

Gordon had been alive then—Gordon, who had been the initial cause of all the unhappiness.

It was the night of the ball in Johannesburg. She could see herself in her glittering white Victorian dress. And Shane meeting her in the moonlit garden; sweeping her off her feet, kidnapping her, gloriously, recklessly under the very nose of her husband. He had carried her off up the mountains to that shooting-box. And they had stayed there. And the sheer beauty of those few days until Gordon had found them. Days of perfect companionship—days when she felt herself utterly at one with him, even though physically she had re-mained chaste.

She went back there to-night, with the aching torment of love for him still in her heart—with the mood upon her that she must give herself wholly to the thought of him, the memory of him—on this the last night she would be alone and free.

A great wave of melancholy seized her when at last she stepped from the car and stood before the pine-log cabin. She had found it with some diffi-culty. But here it was—stark—deserted—rather ghostly with the moon shining down on the roof, and the tall pines like dark sentinels gravely guard-ing it.

She peered through one of the casements and caught a shadowy glimpse of the stove they had lit together—of the sofa covered with a leopard-skin where she had sat, before a leaping fire, in the circle of his arm.

She raised her white young face to the skies.

'Oh, stars—*you* know,' she whispered. 'You know my sorrow.'

Then the silence of the night up in the still, shadowy mountains was broken by the roar of a powerful engine.

Evelyn's heart seemed to stop beating. *For she knew that was the engine of Shane's racing car.*

The same impulse that had brought her up here to-night had brought him too. Instinct had led them both to revisit the spot where they had known the greatest happiness together

It made her realise how united they were, in spite of all the hideous barriers.

XXVI

When Shane's powerful headlamps threw up the slim, dark silhouette of that graceful girl's figure which he knew, at once, to be Evelyn's, an intense joy surged over him. He had come up in the depths of misery, of gloom, of hopeless longing for her. And she, too, had come. Like two passionate devotees they had come to worship at the shrine of love. Alas, it was the tomb of love; for she had signed the death-warrant of their passion when she had sent him from her and chosen Geoffrey Sparnell.

He leaped out of the car. She watched him. He was like a boy, flinging coat and hat on to the running-board, and running toward her, arms outstretched.

Dumbly Evelyn walked into those arms.

Shane held her close—close—his heart beating madly against her own. He put his cheek against hers and felt the salt wet of her tears. Neither of them moved or spoke for a long while, neither did they kiss. But at last he lifted his head and said:

'Sweetheart—Sweetheart—you've come back to me.'

Then she put her arms about his neck and clung to him in wild grief.

'No, Shane, my darling, no. Only for a few hours. I haven't changed my mind about—to-morrow. I can't. I've given my word. And it's better so.'

'Better that you should give to another man all that belongs to me?'

'I shall give nothing that belongs to you, really,' she whispered. Her delicate fingers threaded through his thick dark hair. 'My darling—the physical means so little. My mind, my heart, my soul are yours for ever. What does it matter if Geoffrey has my miserable body?'

'It's such a beautiful, darling body, and I love it as much as I love your beautiful mind.' He laughed, but the laugh might have been a sob, and he would have wept if he had been a woman. Hungrily he kissed her now—long, burning kisses that made her eyelids close and her whole being swim with ecstasy.

'Darling, darling, *darling*,' he said between those wild kisses. 'Can he make you tremble in his arms as you tremble in mine? Will you ever love him as you've loved me? Sweetheart—it isn't possible.'

'I know,' she said. 'Shane, you're right. I never will love him as I love you.'

'Then come away with me now—let's abandon everything—get into my car—drive to the ends of the earth.'

She shivered violently in his arms. The intoxication of Shane in such a mad mood—of Shane's caresses! Dear life, how was she going to refuse him? She was seized, fleetingly, with a desire as crazy as his own to abandon all. To break her word to Geoff; to follow this man to the world's end.

He picked her right up in his arms.

His brown, strong face—radiant with his passion—was as splendid as a god's in the white moonlight. His eyes, darkly blue, almost black, laughed down into hers.

'Can he pick you up—hold you like this, beloved?'

'Oh, darling, don't!' she said weakly.

But with his lips against her mouth, he carried her into the log-cabin, and, in the darkness, laid her on the leopard-skin and knelt beside her, covering her with caresses.

'Mine—mine—mine,' he murmured.

Half swooning, she lay there, locked in his embrace. Then, with a gigantic effort, she pushed him away from her.

'Shane, I ask you—I beg you—to stop—to let me go,' she said breathlessly. 'It's killing me.'

He put his hot lips to her slim pale hands. He whispered softly a quotation of Swinburne's that he had whispered often before:

' *"Where his lips wounded, there his lips atone."* Darling, forgive me if I hurt you. I love you so.'

'You haven't hurt me—that way,' she panted. 'It's my heart that hurts so.'

'Then let me have your heart, beloved.'

'You have always had it,' she said. 'But, Shane, I can't go away with you and you mustn't tempt me so terribly.'

He grew quiet. Her eyes, straining through the darkness of the cabin, saw his face grow white and bitter again.

'After all this—you still mean to marry *him*?'

'Yes, I must. And you must go back to *her*.'

'If you knew how I hate her, Evelyn.'

'But there is the baby.'

'Yes, if it were not for that, nothing would keep me from you.'

'Nor me from you,' she said desolately. 'But it is the child that separates us, Shane.'

He was silent for a long while. Then she put her arms about him with desperate tenderness.

'Don't grieve too much—don't, darling. Let's both try and face it.' The tears poured down her cheeks. 'Let's stay here just a little while together —and have one more beautiful and perfect memory to help us through.'

'Through the rest of life,' he said.

'Yes,' she whispered. 'Try, darling—to help me —because I'm very weak and tired.'

He drew her close to him, kissing her gently now, anguished for her, as well as for himself.

They sat together, like two children, clasping one another, mute and helpless in their misery. Only the moon and the stars, piercing the gloom of that deserted mountain hut, witnessed the tragedy of it.

A little peace came to them, a little resignation, when at last they said good night and good-bye.

'All our lives we'll remember—to-night,' she whispered when she stood in his arms for their last kiss.

But Shane could not speak. He was ashamed of the tears that wet his lashes. He could only kiss her dumbly and wish, with despair in his soul, that to-night had never ended.

They went back to Johannesburg down the quiet dim mountains in their separate cars. And of the two of them perhaps Evelyn was more resigned. But Shane returned to his wife, hating her more violently than ever. She had wronged him unpardonably, and even for the unhappy child's sake he could not forgive her.

He slept ill that night. It was still a festering sore in his very soul that to-morrow Evelyn would become Geoffrey Sparnell's wife.

But she had asked him to be 'kind to Vicky,' and because she had asked it, he rose that day of Evelyn's wedding with every intention of 'being kind' to his wife, even though he could be nothing more.

He was up early and went out riding in the

beautiful South African sunrise. When he came in he bathed, changed from his riding-kit into a white linen suit, and asked one of the servants where the 'missus' was. The boy answered that Mrs. Cargill was in her bedroom and that the doctor was with her.

Shane strolled along to his wife's room. The doctor! Perhaps that meant she was not well. His intention to be kind to Vicky increased. He would get another opinion on her. He disliked the fellow, Dr. Van Olsten, whom she had been having. He was half Dutch, and not one of the medical men whom most of the European residents in Johannesburg called in. He had never understood why she had gone to Van Olsten, but he had been so indifferent he had not expostulated. But he would ask her, to-day, to have an English physician instead of that swarthy, smooth-tongued fellow.

Vicky's bedroom door, which was ajar, swung open in the draught as Shane neared it. Then he heard her low voice—a rather amused, vicious laugh accompanying it.

'Oh, yes, he still thinks I'm having a chi-ild.'

Shane stood still, rooted to the spot, white under his healthy tan. What in God's name did she mean? The voice continued:

'Thanks to you, dear doc, for your excellent help and that report you gave him; but as soon as this other woman is safely married to her new flame, I shall tell Shane I'm not in that condition.'

Shane seemed to turn ice-cold. *Not in that condition.* Vicky was *not* having a child at all. Oh, God!

Then the Dutchman's guttural voice:

'Telling the hubby so has parted him effectively from his woman, *hein*?'

'Yes, quite. And now, how much do I owe you?'

'Oh, a few hundreds will settle my account, dear lady—when you can get a nice little cheque from him.'

'I shan't say a word, mind you, till later in the day. Mrs. Veriland is being married at half-past ten this morning,' came Vicky's voice.

Shane put a hand to his forehead. It was wet. He trembled violently. His eyes had a wild look. His thoughts were chaotic. Every kindly feeling towards his wife was wiped out. He stood there in possession of her vile secret—knowing her foul duplicity—realising that she and the doctor had conspired to deceive him. *That* was why she had chosen the dirty Boer physician. *That* was what she had done—paid him—promised him 'a few hundreds' to endorse her story that she was enceinte. And it was untrue. He, like any man might be, had been absolutely taken in—forced to believe what she and her doctor had told him.

The one and only reason why he had parted from Evelyn, weeks ago, had been because he believed in the existence of his child. That was the only reason Evelyn had sent him from her; why they had parted in grief, in abiding passion, last night.

Something in Shane seemed to snap.

He groaned. He heard Vicky say:

'Ssh—someone—perhaps my husband is coming.'

He did not go into that bedroom. He did not dare, otherwise he knew he would have choked the life out of that vile, scheming woman and Van Olsten as well.

He turned and rushed out of the house like a madman. He got into his car. It was standing there in the sunshine. He had meant to take Vicky shopping. He drove at a furious pace to the registry office where, at half-past ten, Evelyn was to be married to Geoffrey Sparnell. The sweat poured down his ghastly face. He kept laughing insanely. It was funny! It was a jest—a pretty grim one, too. All the parting, the agony, had been for nothing. Vicky was not the mother of his child. There was no reason why he should not take Evelyn away.

But was it too late?

The clocks in the town, one by one, were striking half-past ten.

Black rage—almost murder—stalked the soul of Shane Cargill when he was hung up in a traffic jam in the congested part of the shopping area through which he had to pass to get to the registrar's.

Now, *now*—after what he had found out—if he could not take Evelyn away—something terrible would happen. He had stood too much.

He reached the registry office and swung himself out of the car. He was breathing hard and his eyes burnt in his deathly face. He was hatless, coatless, a strange, wild figure.

He only reached the door of the office, then fell back. Two people came out. A slim, fair-haired, exquisitely pretty woman in a white dress with a big white hat on her golden head. A man in smart grey, with a white carnation in his buttonhole, followed. The man was smiling, radiant. The girl thoughtful, a little sad.

Shane saw them and a mist of red seemed to come across his eyes.

Eve and Sparnell. And—obviously they were married. He was too late.

He shook with crazy laughter. He damned Vicky—damned her soul—her body—her memory—everything about her.

Evelyn, seeing him stand there, white and demented, stared at him in amazement and dismay. Why was he here, looking like this, when he had promised, after their beautiful night in the mountains, never to see her again? It wasn't fair. She had steeled herself for the ordeal of her marriage. He had come to upset her over again.

'Shane!' she said reproachfully.

Geoffrey Sparnell, now Evelyn's husband, came up and took her arm possessively.

'Come along, darling.'

Then Shane, with passion and rage sending him mad, rushed up and wrenched them apart.

'No, by God! I'll not stand for it.'

'Shane!' she cried.

'Listen, Eve, I have discovered that Vicky is not having a child—that she deceived me on purpose to separate us. There is no earthly reason why I should stick to her now. Oh, *God*, don't you understand?'

Shane broke off, panting, ghastly. Evelyn, white-lipped, shaken from her composure, stared up at him with great, startled eyes.

'Oh, no, it can't be true!' she whispered.

'It is true,' said Shane. 'And now, I say, nothing *shall* separate us—not even your marriage to Sparnell.'

Before the amazed Geoffrey could speak, Shane picked Evelyn up in his arms and carried her to the car. A few children, thinking he was the bridegroom, cheered him feebly. Evelyn, like a dumb creature, made no resistance. Shane lifted her into the car and took his seat beside her.

'Now, my Eve—for good and all—and to hell with the world,' he said crazily.

She said nothing. The big car shot forward. She

felt the earth rocking round her. But Shane had not reckoned on the force of Geoffrey Sparnell's jealous fury. Sparnell was in his own car, following, and something small and bright flashed in his right hand. The next moment there was a report. Evelyn turned her head, saw Geoffrey, and screamed. Then Shane, with a broken laugh and a cry of 'Eve!' crumpled up over the steering-wheel.

XXVII

Evelyn's memory of the terrible accident that followed that shot, which had been fired, in a fit of uncontrollable jealousy, by Geoffrey Sparnell, was ever afterwards a vague one. It all happened so swiftly to be clearly recalled.

She did just remember seeing Geoffrey's furious face; the flash of his revolver in the sunlight; and hearing the sound of the report as he fired. She remembered too the horror of watching Shane's big figure crumple up over the steering-wheel of their racing car.

Then came disaster. They were travelling at forty miles an hour. The moment Shane's hands left the steering-wheel the car swerved violently to the right. They crashed into a lamp-standard. Evelyn was conscious only of the violent percussion, heard the ghastly sound of splintering wood and glass, and the hoarse shouting of a man. Then darkness and oblivion.

It was as well for her that she could not see the ghastly aftermath of that crash. For Geoffrey Sparnell, swerving to avoid a collision with the wreckage of Shane's car, lying there a tortured heap on the kerb, met a lorry—head on. There was another frightful crash—a double calamity, and for the unfortunate young man a far worse accident than Shane's. He was the victim of his own crazy jealousy. When they lifted him out of his smashed and broken saloon he was a still figure; horribly still; the white flower in his buttonhole dyed with ominous red; his fair hair dabbled with blood, eyes closed. No whimper or protest came from the pale lips of Evelyn's ill-fated bridegroom when the ambulance arrived and he was put gently on to a stretcher and swung into the vehicle.

A whisper went round the shocked crowd which had gathered around the scene of the double calamity:

'He is dead.'

But from Shane Cargill's lips, when they pulled him away from the twisted steering-wheel which had pinned him down, came at once a question:

'The—the lady with me—is she all right?'

A policeman leaned over him:

'The lady is quite unhurt, sir—miracle—she's only fainted. A very lucky escape.'

Relief mixed with the grimace of pain that twisted Shane's brown face.

'Thank God.'

He refused to enter an ambulance. He was not so badly hurt as they had first imagined. He was severely bruised and cut about the hands, but it was obvious, once he struggled on to his feet, that there were no internal injuries. Blood poured from his left forearm. But that was the flesh-wound Geoffrey's bullet had made. Shane inwardly cursed himself as he stood there on the pavement in the centre of a gaping crowd, allowing the ambulance men to bind up his arm.

'If I hadn't been fool enough to faint, this accident would never have happened,' he said, white and grim.

Evelyn, in the hands of a hospital nurse and a woman doctor who was on the spot, needed no bandaging. She was not cut at all; merely shocked and dazed by the collision. A draught of brandy from the doctor's flask and she was perfectly able to answer the questions a police officer put to her. She avoided mentioning the shot that her husband had fired, and for the time being—there being no eye-witness of the actual shooting—it was merely thought to be an ordinary accident.

Evelyn's feelings when she saw Geoffrey's covered figure driven away in the ambulance were beyond expression. She felt physically sick and ashamed to the core of her being that this thing had happened. She blamed herself.

'I'm morally responsible,' she thought. 'I ought not to have married that poor boy. A few hours ago he was happy, healthy, with a future in front of him. Now, perhaps, his life is ended. Through Shane's folly—and mine.'

She loved Shane too much to attach the blame to him entirely. But Shane reproached himself, as remorseful in his fashion as Evelyn was in hers. When they faced each other on the pavement, both white and shaken, they could not voice their thoughts. Dumbly Evelyn looked up at her lover. Dumbly he returned her gaze. Then with a great effort he whispered:

'Thanks be to God you are not hurt, my darling.'

The tears welled into her eyes. She whispered back:

'And that you are not seriously hurt. But *Geoffrey*——'

'It's all my fault. I went crazy,' he said under his breath. 'I ought to have left you alone. But when I found out that Vicky—well, you know—it just sent me mad to think I'd lost you by a few minutes.'

She nodded. She understood. It had happened to her once—it had been the other way round then. But she remembered how crazy she had felt. It was all such a ghastly tangle. They seemed to flounder more hopelessly than ever, now, after this terrible accident.

A hired car took Shane and Evelyn away from the scene of wreckage.

'I must go to the hospital,' Evelyn said. 'Geoffrey and I were only married half an hour ago. It's too awful. I must go to him.'

Shane made no effort to detain her.

'Of course you must go,' he said. 'I'll come with you and get this infernal arm dressed.'

In the car Evelyn was on the verge of breaking down. Shaking, colourless, she sat huddled in her corner, trying desperately not to lose her control. He forgot that he was an injured man and bruised in every part of his body. He thought only of her. Stricken with remorse, he held tightly on to her cold, nervous fingers.

'Don't lose your courage. Buck up, my darling. You must keep going—you've so much to face.'

She nodded and leaned her head against the cushioned back of the car as they drove slowly to the General Hospital. Shane's heart was wrung for her. She looked so frail and tired—like a very young girl with her fair hair tumbled about her white little face and her delicate white organdie dress torn and dust-stained. She had left her hat, crumpled and ruined, in the wrecked car.

When he remembered her as she had emerged from the registry office, cool, serene, hoping to find contentment with her young husband, and realised that he had done this thing to her, he suddenly groaned and hid his face in his hands.

'I've brought you nothing but misery—tragedy —Eve. I shall never, never forgive myself for this,' he said hoarsely.

She immediately sought to comfort him and put a trembling hand on his hair.

'Shane, dearest, don't blame yourself. I was as much to blame—for marrying Geoffrey. I thought it would be for the best, but I see now that it was wrong to him, to you, to myself.'

'I reproach myself for the whole appalling thing,' he said bitterly.

'No—don't. I must share the blame. But poor Geoffrey can't be blamed for his jealousy. Any other man might have done the same under such provocation.'

'I agree,' said Shane.

'Therefore, whatever our personal feelings are, we must think of Geoffrey now,' she said.

'Yes,' said Shane.

His fingers, roughly bandaged by the ambulance men, fumbled for a cigarette. It was Evelyn who found his case and lit one for him. She put it between his lips.

'You're in pain, my darling?'

'I'm all right. It's nothing——'

'Oh, why, why did it all happen?' she moaned.

He smoked fiercely.

'We've had the devil's own luck from the very beginning. One disaster after another. God knows all we asked was peace—and each other. Eve, imagine my feelings when I discovered this morning that I need not have stood by Vicky—that I could have gone away with you—after all?'

'How did you find out? I don't understand——'

He told her about the Dutch doctor and Vicky's effort to trick him into staying with her. Evelyn's heart beat fast with bitter resentment when she heard:

'It was vile beyond words, my poor Shane.'

'You see,' he said hoarsely. 'We need not have made any sacrifices for her—for the child which never existed. And I tried to get to you in time. It was more than I could stand—to see you married to Sparnell.'

'I understand,' she said brokenly. 'But the consequences of it all are, perhaps, fatal.'

'Was Sparnell very badly hurt? I couldn't see.'

'Neither could I. But they told me he was badly hurt. He had a head-on collision with a lorry—trying to avoid us,' she said, shuddering.

Shane closed his eyes. He felt ill, badly shaken; and his arm was stinging furiously. Wearily he thought:

'If Sparnell dies I shall hold myself responsible. God, what a frightful mess-up—all of it!'

They reached the hospital and separated there.

'I shall go to the out-patient casualty dressing-place,' Shane told Evelyn. 'You'll want to stay with Sparnell, of course.'

'Yes, if I'm wanted,' she said in a low voice.

He gave her a long look of desperate love and remorse.

'Forgive me, Eve.'

'I understand,' she whispered.

'You're an angel.'

'I'll see you to-night. At my hotel—unless you are too bad to come out, then I'll come and see you.'

'Very well,' he said.

She followed the tall, dishevelled figure with her

aching eyes as she walked into the cool white corridors of the hospital.

'How I have loved him,' she thought. 'How I love him still! There can never be anybody else. Yes, I blame myself—for marrying poor Geoff.'

The passion of these two men for her—and of Gordon before them—had caused all these dreadful disasters.

'I mustn't be a fatal person,' she thought, 'destined to bring sorrow to those who care for me. What a terrible thing.'

Then, a few minutes later, when she sat beside the bed in the private ward to which Geoffrey had been taken, she concentrated entirely upon him. He was unconscious, his head swathed in a capelline bandage, the white bedclothes drawn in stiff hospital fashion up to his chin. His terrible immobility frightened her.

'When will he move—when will he open his eyes?' she asked.

'We don't quite know,' the nurses told her gently. 'He is suffering from a wound in the back of the head and concussion. We must just watch and hope.'

'Is he very bad?'

'Rather bad, I am afraid. His pulse is so weak.'

Evelyn sat still, staring at the quiet figure. And she thought, as Shane had done:

'If he dies, I shall be responsible.'

They allowed her to remain. She had some food and a brandy-and-soda. She was still suffering from shock. But she thought of nothing but the unconscious man in the bed. Not for a single instant did she dwell on the idea that she would be free if he died, free to go to Shane. Her one desire was for Geoffrey to recover, because she felt that she and

Shane had caused this terrible thing to happen to him.

William Sparnell, Geoffrey's uncle and owner of The Summer Garden, on receipt of a wire from Evelyn, rushed from Natal to his nephew's bedside. The boy was his heir and a great favourite. He was distracted with worry when he realised the seriousness of Geoffrey's condition, and instructed the doctors and nurses to spare no expense to save him.

He was a little piqued to find Geoffrey married. Geoffrey had kept quite quiet about his passion for Gordon Veriland's lovely widow. But he lost his heart to the golden-haired girl, with her beautiful, tragic eyes, as soon as he saw her.

'It's bad luck—on your wedding-day, my dear,' he said. 'But the boy will get better. He must.'

Evelyn felt more than ever remorseful because of old Sparnell's kindness.

Geoffrey did not recover consciousness that day. When night came he was still insensible. Evelyn was told to go home.

'We will send for you as soon as he is conscious,' the nurses told her.

Evelyn, heavy-hearted and exhausted after the physical and mental ordeal through which she had passed, returned to her rooms, which she had left, believing it to be for good this morning, when she married Geoffrey. Her landlady prepared the room for her—this time in the name of Mrs. Sparnell.

Geoffrey's wife—yet no wife. And the bridegroom in a critical condition in the hospital. The tragedy of it!

Shane came to see her, his arm in a sling, his cuts properly bandaged and attended to. He looked so white, so drawn, that Evelyn would not let him stay more than a few minutes with her.

'You must go home—at once.'

'I haven't been home since the accident,' he said heavily. 'I've been at my club. I don't feel I can face—that creature who is—God help me—both my cousin and my wife.'

Evelyn winced.

'But you must go, my dear. You need rest and sleep. I'm sure you have a fever.'

'A touch of it,' he said indifferently. 'But it's nothing. Sparnell is still unconscious?'

'Yes—they are worried about him.'

'Heaven forgive me, Eve.'

'Oh, don't go on reproaching yourself. So many extenuating circumstances are responsible for the whole disaster!' she cried. Then she reached up her arms to him like a frightened child. 'Shane, Shane, what can we do about it now?'

He held her for a moment—not in passion, but in tenderness, smoothing the silky amber head.

'My poor sweet love, there is nothing to do now but to wait and let the tangle unravel itself.'

'If ever it does!' she said piteously.

'Yes, if ever it does,' he repeated, and looked with grim eyes over the beautiful golden head which he was stroking.

When he left her, he forced himself to go back to his own place. He was a sick man himself and he needed rest and oblivion.

He hoped that Vicky would not be there. But she was waiting for him, anxiously pacing up and down their private sitting-room. All day, all the evening, she had waited, wondering what had happened to him and why he had been absent all day. She had not the vaguest idea that he had overheard the conversation between her and Dr. Van Olsten.

She was still, in her fashion, crazy about Shane

and frightened that she might lose him. She meant to make herself very attractive to him when he did come home. She wore one of her loveliest dresses— deep midnight blue, with big dark blue stones glittering round her white neck.

But Shane, when he walked wearily into the room, did not even notice what she wore or what she looked like. He only knew that he despised and hated her.

Vicky gave a frightened look at his grim face and bandaged arms and fingers.

'Good heavens! What happened, Shane?'

'You haven't seen the evening paper, then?' he asked drily.

'No—why? What has happened? An accident?'

'An accident, yes,' he said grimly. 'For which I hold you, in a way, responsible.'

She put a hand to her lips.

'Shane—what do you mean?'

'I mean this'—now his voice cut like a whip. 'I found out everything—the whole dirty, lying, loathesome game that you've been playing—the whole foul bargain that you struck with that Dutch snake, Van Olsten!'

Vicky's face turned a grey shade. Her heart seemed to stop beating, then race madly with fear and dismay.

'Shane—I—you——'

'Don't bother to make any excuses,' he broke in. 'I won't listen to them. I know that you are not the mother of my child and never have been. This is the end. I'm quitting—to-morrow morning. We're going to have a divorce, and as long as I live I shall never forgive you and never see your treacherous face again.'

Vicky, aghast, stupefied that he had found her out, began to cry.

'Shane—I love you——'

But he put his fingers to his ears, brushed her aside, and walked out of the room. When she followed, she found his bedroom door locked against her, and neither protests, pleas, nor hysterics could make him unlock it.

Then Vicky knew that it was indeed the end and that her sins had found her out.

While Shane was still sleeping, early that next morning, she telephoned to Van Olsten.

'My husband knows everything,' she said sullenly. 'He's going to insist on a divorce. It means *finis* to our arrangement.'

'And what will happen to you?'

'I don't know and I don't care,' she said bitterly.

'You know how I feel about you, Vicky,' came his eager voice. 'Would you like to join me—in Dutch East? I'm thinking of going there—to some wealthy relatives of mine. I would like to introduce you as—the future Mrs. Van Olsten.'

Vicky's cheeks crimsoned. For one genuinely unhappy moment she thought of Shane, whom she had lost so irrevocably. Then she shrugged her shoulders. She liked Hans Van Olsten. He was a genial person; clever; sure to make money; and he had extremely wealthy relatives in Dutch East Africa. That sounded good. Why, after all, should she languish in Johannesburg alone?

'I'll come,' she said.

'Good. *Ich liebe dich*,' he said in German.

She rang off.

XVIII

Geoffrey Sparnell did not recover consciousness for forty-eight hours. During that time Evelyn, stricken with remorse, scarcely left his bedside. She was anxious to do her level best to please him, to make reparation, when he awoke.

Shane, respecting her feelings, made no further attempt to see her. She was grateful for his consideration, and sent him a small note, telling him that she would see him later on.

Then Geoffrey Sparnell came out of the shadows, and although pulse and heart were feeble and his condition still critical, he recognised Evelyn and spoke to her.

'Grey-Eyes—darling,' were his first words.

She bent over the bed, laying her cool hand on his fevered ones.

'Geoff—my dear!'

'Love you,' he said in a blurred voice, and closed his eyes again.

Evelyn called for the nurse.

'Oh, is he all right? He's just spoken to me—recognised me.'

'He'll open his eyes and speak to you again, no doubt,' was the reassuring answer. 'He's very weak, and concussion's a tricky thing.'

Geoffrey did open his eyes and speak again—much later that same day. This time he seemed much more himself and his voice stronger. He clung to Evelyn and seemed unable to bear her out of his sight.

'Rotten bad luck—crashing in the car,' he said feebly. 'Can't remember—how it happened.'

Evelyn's heart missed a beat. Her cheeks flushed and paled again.

'Can't you—remember anything, Geoff?'

He touched his bandaged forehead gingerly.

'Remember—getting tied up—to sweetest woman in the world.'

The tears started to her eyes.

'Yes, dear—we were married. And after that?'

'Nothing—but—the crash.'

She swallowed hard. So the concussion had affected his memory. He made no mention of Shane—of the shooting episode. He just imagined they had had an unfortunate accident in his own car when they were driving away on their honeymoon.

'Such a mercy you weren't hurt, darling,' he whispered, holding weakly on to her hands.

Evelyn saw clearly where the path of duty lay, and she followed it without hesitation. Geoff must be left in ignorance of what had really happened. Shane's name must not come into it.

'You must hurry up and get well, my dear,' she said very gently, and stooped and laid her lips upon his.

'Ah—that's good,' he whispered, and smiled. 'How sweet your hair smells, Evelyn.'

'Get well,' she repeated chokily.

'Then we'll have our honeymoon eh?'

'Yes, yes—indeed.'

'My wife,' he whispered, and closed his eyes again.

'I shouldn't talk any more,' the nurse whispered in Evelyn's ear. 'His pulse is so bad.'

'But he will get well now?'

'I hope and believe so.'

Evelyn left the hospital, her state of mind quite chaotic. She was glad—terribly glad her husband would get well. She would, of course, go away with him and commence married life as soon as he was fit again. But Shane was left—Shane would be alone—the odd man out in this tragedy. And he loved her. How utterly he had proved that!

No more than she loved him—would always love

him. But this time she must not falter; neither of them must make a protest. They must renounce each other finally.

She sent for Shane that evening. He came with a queer look in his handsome eyes which made her at once question him!

'What has happened, Shane?'

'Vicky has left me,' he said.

'Left you?'

'Yes. We had things out last night. I told her I had discovered her vile intrigue with Dr. Van Olsten. She left Johannesburg with him this morning. They have gone to Dutch East—and she wants a divorce.'

'I see,' said Evelyn.

She walked to her sitting-room window and looked out at the starry African night. Her lips twisted ironically. So Shane would be free now. And what use? Surely fate had been unnecessarily cruel.

Shane looked hungrily at her.

'What now, my dearest?'

'Nothing—but a parting,' she said with a break in her voice. She turned and gave him her hands blindly: 'Geoffrey is better. He remembers nothing about you and the shooting. He only knows that we—were married. As soon as he is better I am going away with him.'

Shane bowed his head. He held the little hands so tightly that he hurt his own sore, injured fingers, but he was unconscious of the pain.

'Well—that ends things finally, Eve.'

'Yes,' she whispered.

'I've nothing to say except that I wish you—luck and happiness, and I want you to forgive me for all the trouble I've brought you and to remember that

I loved you and still love you more than life itself.'

The tears blinded her.

'Shane, Shane, I know, and I've nothing to forgive. You've brought me so much more happiness than sorrow. Darling, darling, Shane, I shall never love any man as I love you, and I shall remember what has passed between us till I die.'

With an effort he refrained from sweeping her passionately to his heart and kissing those lovely lips again and again. But she was not for him, and he controlled his passion. He kissed both her hands.

'Good-bye, my Sweet. Life's been horribly cruel —unbelievably so—to both of us. But—try and be happy. Good-bye.'

She did not answer. She was crying desperately now. He left her while he had the strength to do so. She thought despairingly:

'I shall never see him again. It's like death to me!'

But she must live on—for poor Geoffrey's sake.

She felt that night that her love-life, at least, was ended, and that when Shane left her he took the whole of her heart with him.

Towards dawn the next morning she was sent for urgently by the hospital authorities. Mr. Sparnell, they said, had taken a turn for the worse. His temperature had gone right up during the night and then dropped perilously low. He seemed to have recovered his memory absolutely and was asking for her.

With heavy heart Evelyn rushed to her husband's bedside. When she sat beside him, she knew at once that he was not going to live. In the pearly light of the beautiful South African dawn, Geoffrey Sparnell's face was the colour of wax and his features looked unnaturally sharpened. He had been given a stimulant. He spoke to her quite clearly, but his eyes were queer—glassy.

Evelyn, with fear in her soul, took both his hands.

'Dearest Geoff—you want me?'

'Yes,' he said. 'I've remembered—everything.'

'I wish you had not,' she said.

'But I'm glad, in a way. Grey-Eyes—I'm dying.'

'No,' she said. 'Oh, no—it isn't true.'

He smiled strangely.

'It's true. I feel it. And I'm glad I realise everything—so that I can—apologise to you.'

'But it's Shane and I who owe the apology,' she said, and had difficulty in restraining her tears.

'Listen, dear,' said Geoffrey Sparnell in a curiously detached voice, as though he had already dissociated himself from affairs of this world. 'I fired that shot at Cargill—in a fit of damned silly rage and jealousy. I am entirely responsible, and I am thankful to God that he is all right—and that you are unhurt. The nurses told me all about it.'

'Shane is so sorry,' she whispered, and the tears fell thick and fast despite her efforts to stem the tide of them. 'But he was terribly provoked, Geoff. He found that his wife had betrayed him and that she was not the mother of his child at all.'

'So that's it,' said Geoffrey, nodding.

'Yes.'

'Poor chap. I'm sorry for him. No—I need not be sorry. He'll have you now.'

'No, no—what are you saying, Geoff?'

'I tell you I'm dying, Eve.'

'Please, don't!' she said, in an agony of mind.

'It's the best way out of the tangle. You and Cargill have had bad luck. I want you to join him now—and be happy at last, my poor darling.'

Evelyn could not speak. His generosity overwhelmed her. Then, when she saw a change come over his face, she called the nurse in terror.

A doctor was sent for—a cylinder of oxygen—Evelyn was taken away from Geoffrey's bedside.

They came to her later and told her gravely that he was dead.

'His heart failed. His pulse was so bad after his temperature dropped. We rather feared——' the doctor said, gently, when he broke the news to Evelyn.

She stared stonily ahead of her. Her tragic eyes were dry now of tears. She knew no pleasure in her freedom; only immeasurable pity for the young life cut down in its prime, and terrible remorse for the part that she and Shane had played in the tragedy.

Old Sparnell, grief-stricken at the loss of his nephew and heir, took Evelyn home. He did not like the look of her. She was ghastly, and her eyes had a haunted expression.

'My dear, you mustn't grieve too much,' he said. 'Geoff wouldn't have wished it, and you were only married a few hours. Time heals these things.'

She thought dumbly:

'He doesn't understand! I blame myself—so terribly. I can't believe Geoffrey is dead. There are things. Time can never heal.'

But later, when the first terrible shock passed, she thought of Shane, whom she loved so well and from whom she had parted finally.

'Why doesn't he come? He must have seen in the papers that Geoffrey died,' she told herself.

But that black day passed—and another day and another night—then Geoffrey Sparnell's funeral—and still Shane made no sign—sent no word—and made no effort to see her.

Two days after poor Geoffrey Sparnell had been laid in his last resting-place Evelyn decided that she must see Shane, if only once again.

They had parted finally. But that had been because of Geoffrey. Why Shane had not come to her or sent even a word of sympathy she could not understand. She was afraid that he might be ill.

Deep though her remorse might be and lasting her grief for the unhappy young man who had loved her so disastrously, her tired heart yearned for her lover.

Old Sparnell went back to Natal, after insisting upon making Evelyn financially comfortable, for his nephew's sake. Evelyn went round to the hotel wherein she knew Shane had been staying.

They told her there that he had gone to his club.

At the club she was informed that Mr. Cargill had left Johannesburg some days ago.

Evelyn's heart seemed to fail her.

'When did he actually leave?' she asked.

They mentioned the date, and then she understood. It was the day on which Geoffrey had died. He must have gone long before the newspapers could chronicle the death of the young manager of The Summer Garden, following the terrible accident on his wedding-day.

'Can you tell me where to find him?' Evelyn asked the manager of Shane's club.

He looked curiously at the pale, slender girl in the black georgette dress and big black hat—so lovely in spite of her mourning—like a lily, golden-crowned.

'I'm awfully sorry,' he said. 'I can't possibly put

you in touch with Mr. Cargill. He said he was off on a big-game hunt with a Major Forsyth and a Mr. Beaconsfield. He asked me to keep all letters here, as he would be in the wilds of Tanganyika. He thought he would be away at least a year.'

Evelyn came out of the club, her spirits at zero. Away a whole year! And he did not know that she was alone—free from all shackles once again. Was Fate to continue playing these ironic jests—to the bitter end?

She needed Shane now, she wanted frantically to see him and tell him that Geoffrey's dying wish had been that they should find happiness together.

What possible chance was there of getting into touch with him?

Then a forlorn hope seized her. He might be at his shooting-box in the mountains—might have gone there to collect his rifles and kit.

A slender chance; but she acted on impulse, and changing her thin mourning dress for a white linen suit, drove in her small car up to that well-remembered and well-loved spot which all her life she would connect with Shane and the most passionate happiness she had ever known.

It so happened that three men were sitting outside Shane's log cabin that beautiful evening toward sunset, smoking their pipes and discussing the plans for their trip, when Evelyn arrived on the scene.

Shane and his friends, Major Forsyth and Tom Beaconsfield, were setting out for Tanganyika at dawn the next morning. As Evelyn had hoped, they had come here to collect weapons and kit.

It had been Shane's one idea to go away from the city, escape from his own griefs and worries, and get beyond reach of Evelyn, not that he could for an instant erase the aching need of her from his mind, his heart.

That heart leaped madly when he saw the slim golden-haired girl, in her white suit, step out of her car. Leaving his friends, he rushed to her side and gripped her hands.

'Eve! Oh, my dear, why have you come?'

She looked at him with great shining eyes.

'Shane, I was so afraid you had gone and that I wouldn't find you. Shane—I'm *free.*'

His pulses stirred and his brown face flushed from chin to brow.

'Eve—you mean Sparnell——'

'Is dead. And in dying asked that I should join you.'

Silence. Then Shane said in a low voice:

'God rest him, Eve.'

'Yes,' she whispered.

Then he took her in his arms, and kissed her passionately—thirsty for her sweet lips—and whispered:

'Mine at last—oh, Sweetheart—mine, *mine* at last!'

'For ever, never to be parted this time,' she said, and put her flushed, tear-wet cheek against his brown one in silent ecstasy.

Later Shane approached his very astonished friends, Forsyth and Beaconsfield, and led up to them the most beautiful woman they had ever seen.

'Gentlemen—my future wife,' he said gravely, his handsome eyes shining. 'And I'm afraid I'm going to disappoint you. I can't come with you to-morrow after all.'

'I think I understand,' said Major Forsyth.

'Of course,' murmured Beaconsfield.

'Perhaps you'll come back in six months' time and be witnesses at my wedding,' added Shane.

They shook hands with Evelyn and wished her luck. Later Shane drove her back to her hotel. When his divorce was through he would marry her at once, but meanwhile he was going to take care of her, for was she not the most precious thing in the world to him?

Up in the log cabin two somewhat mystified big-game hunters discussed the affair.

'I knew Cargill was getting a divorce from that red-haired woman, whom I never liked,' said Forsyth. 'But I didn't realise there was another girl in the thing.'

'Obviously there is,' said Beaconsfield. 'And he's a lucky fellow. Did you notice the way she looked at him? Forsyth, she is as beautiful as an angel.'

'Here's jolly good luck to them, anyhow,' said the Major, and solemnly raised his mug of beer.

DENISE ROBINS

FORBIDDEN

Two young lovers seeking the atmosphere of peace and tranquillity they were never able to find in London emerge from a car in a sunlit Provencal town square. It was an idyllic setting for a passionately romantic interlude, but the dazzling light and contrasting deep shadows echoed the pattern of their own life, for Nat was a brilliant young surgeon with a professional reputation to uphold and Toni was married to a vindictive business tycoon.

'Rarely has any writer of our times delved so deeply into the secret places of a woman's heart'

Taylor Caldwell

CORONET BOOKS

ALSO BY DENISE ROBINS
IN CORONET BOOKS

All these books are available at your local bookshop or newsagent, or can be ordered direct from the publisher. Just tick the titles you want and fill in the form below.

Prices and availability subject to change without notice.

CORONET BOOKS, P.O. Box 11, Falmouth, Cornwall.

Please send cheque or postal order, and allow the following for postage and packing:

U.K. — One book 18p plus 8p per copy for each additional book ordered, up to a maximum of 66p.

B.F.P.O. and EIRE — 18p for the first book plus 8p per copy for the next 6 books, thereafter 3p per book.

OTHER OVERSEAS CUSTOMERS — 20p for the first book and 10p per copy for each additional book.

Name...

Address..

....